The Case of the Golden Boy

Books by Eric Wilson

The Tom and Liz Austen Mysteries

Also available by Eric Wilson

The Case of the Golden Boy

A Tom Austen Mystery

by

Eric Wilson

HarperCollins*Publishers*Ltd

As in his other mysteries, Eric Wilson writes here about imaginary people in a real landscape.

First edition: 1994

Cover and chapter illustrations © 1994 by Stephen Snider

Canadian Cataloguing in Publication Data

Wilson, Eric
  The case of the golden boy

(A Tom Austen mystery)
ISBN 0-00-647939-1

I. Title. II. Series: Wilson, Eric. A Tom Austen mystery.

PS8595.I583C 1994   jC813'.54   C94-932261-X
PZ7.W55Ca

---

94 95 96 97 98 99 ❖ OPM 10 9 8 7 6 5 4 3 2

Printed and bound in the United States

For kids everywhere

A note from Eric Wilson

This story is dedicated to kids because you have made my books a success. When I was a teacher and a struggling would-be author, my students urged me to "try again, sir" when I couldn't find a publisher for my stories.

Once I broke into print with *Murder on The Canadian*, kids told each other about the book, starting the "word of mouth" publicity that has built a following for my mysteries over the years.

I listen closely to my readers' comments, and I ask volunteer student editors for their thoughts on each new story as I work on it. So I turned to a grade 6 class at Toronto's Rolph Road School for advice when I thought about publishing, as an artifact, the first Tom Austen adventure I ever wrote. The class enthusiastically said, "Go for it!", so the story is now in print.

Like those students, I hope you will be interested to see the beginning of my evolution as a writer. Here I introduce some familiar characters, as well as people you may recognize from other stories. You'll also detect how I was intrigued enough with some ideas in this story to explore them again later, as I developed as a mystery author.

So, this book is for you, my readers and friends and true supporters. With it, I give you my thanks—from the heart.

Yours mysteriously,

Eric Wilson

1

It was night when Tom Austen and his friends approached the mystery house. "All right," Tom said in a low voice, "are your instructions clear?"

Matthew and Art nodded.

"Any last minute questions?"

None.

"Final check of watches." Tom pulled back his parka sleeve. "Total silence."

He ran his eyes over the deserted house. No signs of life, but he gazed a long time at the attic window. That's where he'd seen movement yesterday. No one had believed it, so Tom proposed a mission into the house. Only Art and Matthew had the courage to come along.

Spring would arrive soon, but the cold of winter still gripped Winnipeg. Branches rattled together in the icy wind, and the black sky was scattered with brilliant stars.

The house had been empty a year. People crossed the street if they had to walk past, and there were rumors of ghosts. Then, yesterday, a dog was barking at the house when Tom went past. Looking up at the attic window, he thought he saw a movement.

Tom motioned for Matthew and Art to stop. "Footprints," he whispered, pointing at a patch of snow. "Coming from the front yard."

"They go to that basement window," Matthew said. "It's been broken."

The window opened easily. The boys dropped down into the cellar. It was dark and smelled of old newspapers. Tom's nose wrinkled. He signaled to Art, who was posted as sentry outside the window. He'd go for help if they weren't back in 15 minutes.

The house moaned. Fear ran across Tom's skin. Another moan, then a long creak that shivered through the darkness. Outside the broken window, Art waited. His breath steamed in the cold air. He looked safe. For a second, Tom wished he was sentry, but he was leader and had to do the hard part.

Switching on their flashlights, they tiptoed to the stairs. As they started up, the house seemed to whisper *Stay away*.

Tom's scalp prickled. He looked at Matthew, wanting desperately to say something, but the rule was no talking. He looked up the stairs, knowing they had to keep going. Tomorrow at school, everyone would be asking questions.

What if someone was waiting upstairs with a gun, planning to spring a trap? Keep Tom and Matthew prisoner in the attic until they starved to death?

Tom stared at Matthew, wishing they could talk. Maybe they should come back another time. What if someone really was lurking with a gun? Maybe it wasn't just his imagination that the house had whispered *Stay away*.

The steps creaked as they climbed from the cellar to the kitchen. Through the dirty windows, Tom saw the sky growing darker. He looked at the old enamel sink, the wooden cupboards, the thick dust on the floor. He heard a scrabbling sound, whirled, and saw a mouse rushing away.

Matthew was trembling. Tom squeezed his friend's arm and tried to smile as they entered the hallway. The plan was for Matthew to wait here as sentry while Tom climbed the dark stairs alone to the attic. That didn't seem like such a good idea anymore.

The house had stopped creaking, as if it was watching and waiting. Tom looked up the stairs.

BANG BANG BANG

The sound crashed down from the darkness. Tom jumped, then Matthew grabbed his arm. "*What was that*?" he whispered.

BANG BANG BANG

The crashing filled the air. Matthew said something and ran; Tom stared up into the darkness, then rushed into the kitchen. He heard Matthew crashing down the cellar stairs. "Art," he was screaming, "help, Art, help!"

Tom flew down the cellar stairs, certain that someone with a gun was close behind. Matthew was wiggling out the window. "Wait for me," Tom yelled, scrambling after him. "Hurry," he shouted, as they ran across the yard. "Hurry!"

When they reached safety, Tom turned to study the deserted house. The attic window stared back, its secret still guarded. Tom promised himself he would return.

"That banging," Matthew gasped. "What was it?"

"I don't know," Tom said.

"What happened in there?" Art demanded. "One minute I'm waiting for you guys and the next minute we're racing across the yard!"

"It was a ghost!" Matthew's eyes were wide. "It made a slamming noise, warning us away."

Tom shook his head. "I don't think it was a ghost, Matthew. But I can tell you one thing—tomorrow we face some tough questioning at school."

"That's right," Matthew exclaimed. He looked at Tom. "What'll we do?"

"It's simple," he replied. "Tell everyone we've got some good leads, and our plans are top secret. Beyond that, *no comment*."

"It makes sense," Art said.

Matthew nodded. "If Dietmar Oban finds out, we're finished. Everyone will be laughing."

Tom looked at his watch. "Fortunately, my parents are away on a trip, but you guys are in trouble. It's getting late."

"Gosh," Matthew exclaimed, looking at his watch. "I'll be grounded for sure."

"Me, too," Art groaned. "Forget the detective business, Tom. It's just plain scary."

Tom shook his head. "No way. I'm on to a good case, I can just tell." When the others looked doubtful, Tom smiled. "Wait and see."

2

The next morning, Tom was reading *The Twisted Claw*—his favorite Hardy Boys mystery—when his sister Liz knocked the milk over. The cold white liquid splashed and gurgled as it rushed across the kitchen table at Tom. He leapt to safety, but the book got soaked.

"Oh, no," he cried. "Now the pages will stick together."

"I'm sorry, Tom."

"Frank and Joe were just entering the hideout of the Pirate King. I need to know what happens next!"

"But you were reading the same book at Christmas," Liz said. "You already know what happens."

"But..." Tom shrugged. "You've got to be in the detective business to understand."

After cleaning up the mess, they talked in the living room with their Uncle Henry, who was staying with them while their parents took a holiday in Mexico. Uncle Henry loved to tell stories about people like his cousin, who lived in a 98-room castle in Toronto.

"He keeps diamonds hidden there," Uncle Henry chuckled. "Can you believe it? Doesn't trust safety deposit boxes—what a character!"

"I'd like to visit that place," Liz said. She polished her eyeglasses. "Always smudged! Some day I'm getting contacts."

Tom opened another Hardy Boys mystery and Liz returned to her book about Green Gables. As they read, a police car pulled up outside. The car door slammed, and a man in uniform came to the door.

"It's Officer Larson," Tom said. "He looks upset."

"I'll get straight to the point," said the grumpy officer. "Some kids broke into the deserted house on Borebank Street. A neighbor saw, and complained to us." He stared at Tom. "My first guess was Tom Austen, playing detective again. Correct?"

Tom nodded solemnly. Liz was silent.

Officer Larson leaned over Tom. "Remember the green creatures from Mars? Remember starting the rumor they had landed?"

Tom's eyes were on the floor.

"When people found green blobs outside their houses, they almost died of shock, thinking the Martians were closing in." Officer Larson shook his head. "But it was only lime ice cream, courtesy of Tom Austen."

* * *

As Tom had predicted to Art and Matthew, a mob of kids surrounded them in the school playground. The sun was stronger today, and parkas were open.

Dietmar Oban was face-to-face with Tom. "I bet you were scared, Austen."

"Not a chance, Oban."

"What happened in the abandoned house?"

"No comment," Tom replied.

Dietmar turned to the other boys. "Did Austen panic in the house? I bet he ran screaming into the night."

"No comment," Matthew said.

"Yeah," Art added. "No comment."

Heads high, the three young detectives went into the school. People asked some more questions, then gave up. *No comment* was all they heard. Tom was satisfied by this damage control, but still felt curious about the old house. He wanted to return, if only to solve the riddle of the terrible banging sound from the attic.

In the hallway, Tom talked to Elizabeth Whitman, a shy girl with friendly eyes and dark hair. Together they were editors of the school newspaper, which this month featured photographs of everyone who worked at Queenston School.

Tom smiled at Elizabeth. "Your pictures are great. I love the one of Mr. Nicholson, frowning."

"Just before I took the picture, I asked him to announce extra school holidays."

As Tom laughed, he saw a man approach. For many years, Pete Tyler had been the school custodian; in all those years, no one had ever seen him smile. He was very tall.

"Hi Pete," Elizabeth said. "Did you like your picture in our newspaper?"

"It was okay," he replied. "But I don't like pictures. Too many bad memories."

"What do you mean?" Tom asked.

"Nothing," the custodian replied, walking away.

Tom and Elizabeth shrugged at each other, then went into their classroom. A few minutes later, Dianne Dorchester arrived, and Tom's heart skipped a beat. She had blond hair and blue eyes, and he often gazed at her across the classroom. The one time she'd caught him staring, Tom had blushed crimson. Today she wore a soft sweater and a plaid skirt.

One of the girls smiled at Dianne. "Where'd you get the tartan skirt? In Scotland?"

She nodded. "My family was there last summer on holiday. It's a neat place."

"Listen, I've often wondered something," the girl said. "Why do you attend Queenston? Your family's so wealthy, you could be in a private school."

"This school's where I want to be," Dianne replied. "My friends are all here."

Their teacher, Mr. Stones, called for order, and announced his plans for a "Kids Day" to celebrate his students. "I'll bring some food," he promised.

"Can we have pizza?" Dianne asked. "It's my favorite."

"Pizza gives me heartburn," Mr. Stones said, "But I'll get some for you, Dianne."

"Thanks, sir!"

They all liked Mr. Stones, who had been a champion basketball player before becoming a teacher. He believed they could do anything in life, and wanted to help them succeed.

The day passed quickly. At 2:45, Mr. Stones looked up from his desk and nodded to Tom and Chuck. "You may go," he said.

Minutes later, Tom had buckled a school-patrol belt over his parka and was standing at the corner of Kingsway and Waterloo, where his job was to stop traffic whenever students wanted to cross. Unfortunately, it wasn't a busy corner and there was little to do, but Tom was very proud of the belt and his authority to stop cars.

A light snow powdered the streets, making the surface slippery. Tom checked the road for Skid Factor by taking several long slides, then waited impatiently.

The first students appeared in the distance. Tom stamped his cold feet and adjusted his belt, ready for business. As usual, he watched in dismay as almost every kid turned off at Queenston and Niagara, giving the patrol on those corners lots of business and Tom nothing.

But then Dianne came his way, the yellow of her parka bright in Tom's eyes. He adjusted his belt again, rubbing the silver buckle to make it glow, then glanced along Waterloo. To his delight, he saw that a pickup truck would reach his corner at the same time as Dianne. At last, he could hold up traffic for her. As she reached his side, Tom stepped into the road. He put up his hand, calmly signaling the driver to stop.

But Tom's timing was bad for such a slippery road. He saw surprise on the driver's face, then shock as he jammed on the brakes and the truck skidded out of control.

It was coming straight at them.

3

Dianne screamed.

Tom threw himself at her. They fell together in the snow as the truck hit the curb and bounced off, spinning in a circle until it stopped in the middle of the street.

Silence. Tom opened his eyes and saw sparkling white crystals of snow. He wondered if he was in heaven, then lifted his head and saw Dianne's blue eyes.

"Are we safe?" she whispered.

"I hope so." Tom was afraid to tell her they might be in heaven. He felt terrible—he shouldn't have tried to stop the truck.

"You crazy kid!"

Tom knew they were alive when he heard the angry driver. He got slowly to his feet.

"You crazy kid!" The driver's face was as red as the curly hair on his head. Despite the cold, he wore jeans and a light jacket displaying the name Red. "You almost got me and Dianne killed! Are you crazy?"

"I'm sorry," Tom said to the man. "Are you going to phone the police?"

"The cops? Not a chance."

Someone opened the door of a nearby house and a big dog ran into the yard. Turning pale with fear, the man immediately got into his pickup truck. The windshield was cracked, and rust stained the fading brown paint. He looked at Tom. "I've seen you before, kid. I live next to the abandoned house on Borebank Street—you were sneaking in with your buddies. That's a scary place to be, especially at night—you've got courage." He paused. "But you're also too snoopy."

Red's eyes stared at Tom. "Stay away from that place, kid. Got that?"

Without waiting for a reply, he gunned the engine and was gone.

Tom pulled out his notebook. "Have you seen that guy before, Dianne?"

"Nope."

"Very interesting," Tom said, jotting this down. "He knew your name. I wonder why?"

*   *   *

That night, Tom stood alone in the cellar of the deserted house and listened to it moan and creak. He felt the same shivering fear, but this time he was determined to get to the attic.

Trying not to listen to the sounds, Tom quickly climbed the cellar stairs. Standing in the front hall, he muffled the glow of his flashlight as he studied the abandoned furniture. There wasn't much, and it was drab.

Tom started upstairs. The landing was thick with dust and it tickled Tom's nose. More stairs led higher, up to the attic.

BANG BANG BANG

The same terrible noise! It roared down the stairs from above. Tom stared up into the darkness, and then began climbing to the attic. His heart thumped in his chest, and his breathing was harsh. The noise continued—BANG BANG BANG—but Tom went higher.

The attic was small and empty. Tom saw a small closet with two wire hangers. The wind blew through the open window, causing venetian blinds to bang against the frame.

"So *that's* the noise," Tom said. "It wasn't a ghost!"

Then he glanced down the stairs. A flashlight shone somewhere below, and he heard the voices of two men.

They were coming his way.

*   *   *

Quickly, Tom looked for a hiding place. The closet was his only hope. He scurried inside, but the door wouldn't close properly. Through the opening, Tom saw the approaching flashlight beam, and then two men entered the room.

One was Red, the driver of the pickup truck. He was smoking a cigarette, and wore the same light jacket and jeans. The second man wore a parka fringed with spiky white fur, and a dark ski mask that covered his head completely. "I don't like this," he said.

Tom leaned forward, straining to hear the low voice. It seemed familiar.

"You'll do as I tell you," Red said angrily, "or your family dies. I've been planning this a long time—you can't back out now. Understood?"

The other man nodded his shrouded head.

Red handed him an envelope. "Your instructions are inside. Memorize them, then burn everything. Our next meeting will be four o'clock Saturday at the Golden Boy."

*   *   *

After school the next day, Dianne stopped to chat with Tom at his school patrol corner. "Any sign of the red-headed man today?"

Tom stared shyly at the ground. "Actually, something did happen." He described the two men meeting at the mystery house. "I'll tell my parents when they get home tonight from their holiday."

"Do you think those men are criminals?"

"Possibly."

Dianne touched his hand. "Don't take any chances, Tom."

"I'll be okay," he replied bravely. "Don't worry about me."

For a moment her blue eyes studied his face. Then she smiled, "Bye, Tom."

"See you." He was too shy to say her name. "Bye." He watched Dianne until a twist of wind hid her yellow parka behind a flurry of snow.

Then, Tom had a strange feeling of foreboding.

He looked toward the school, decided that no more kids would be coming past his corner, and started quickly after Dianne. He knew it was against the rules to leave his post, but something made him want to stay near her. The wind carried the blowing snow into his face as he hurried along Waterloo.

After crossing Academy Road, a busy street with small stores and some traffic lights, Dianne turned into a quiet residential area. Tom continued to follow at a distance, still nagged by fear.

A small brown van pulled out from a side street and approached Dianne, moving quietly through the snow. The windows on the rear doors had been painted over and displayed the words *Blind Driver*; the person at the wheel was hidden from Tom's view.

The van stopped beside Dianne. She looked in the passenger window, which was open.

"Oh, hello! It's nice to see you."

The driver said something that Tom couldn't hear. If he moved closer, Dianne would see that he had followed her like a silly puppy.

"Thank you," Dianne said cheerfully. "A ride would be nice. It's cold today!"

She got inside, and the van pulled away. As Tom walked back to his patrol corner, he was nagged by a strange uneasiness. Although he tried to chase it away, the feeling remained when he reached home and took off his patrol belt. Once again he pictured Dianne getting into the van, and once again he felt sad and lost.

4

"Have you heard!?"

Art was yelling and waving his arms as he ran down the street toward Tom.

"Have you heard!?"

Art stopped in front of Tom, panting, trying to catch his breath.

"Dianne Dorchester is missing!"

Tom stared at Art's face, looking for the grin that would tell him it was a joke, but all he could find was excitement and fear.

"It's true," Art said. "It was on the radio this morning. Dianne is missing! There's police searching for her and everything."

Tom was too shocked to speak. Why Dianne?

Why would anyone want to take Dianne?

"They've got dogs out," Art said, "and they're searching the woods, and they've got roadblocks to stop cars, but they can't find her anywhere!"

But Tom didn't hear Art's words. He was remembering yesterday afternoon, the strange feeling that had made him follow Dianne. The brown van.

"Come on," he called to Art. They ran all the way to school. At the edge of the playground, they stared in awe and horror as three police officers came out of the school and drove off in a car with the emergency lights flashing. Students stood in groups, talking in low voices. Tom told Art and some friends about the brown van, then entered the school alone.

The halls were empty all the way to his classroom. Tom tried not to worry about Dianne, but sadness tugged at his eyes when he saw her empty desk. She sat there just yesterday, he thought, and now she's gone.

"Yes, Tom?" Mr. Stones sat behind his big wooden desk. "What is it?" The morning light through the windows made shadows on his unhappy face.

Tom carefully closed the classroom door. "May I speak to you, sir?"

"Yes, Tom, you may." Usually Mr. Stones spoke with a deep, strong voice, but today it sounded weak and broken. Everyone knew that Dianne was his favorite student, even though he tried to hide it, and Tom felt sorry for him as he approached the desk.

"I have some information," Tom said quietly. "About Dianne."

"*What*?" The teacher's eyes widened. "Do you mean that, Tom?"

"Yes, sir." Even though Tom was upset about Dianne, it was exciting to be part of the drama.

"This isn't one of your jokes?"

"No, sir. I'm serious."

Mr. Stones stood up. "Then let's go to the principal's office. He'll want to phone the police."

"Yes, sir," Tom said.

The linoleum in the hallway was shiny. They walked in silence, and then Tom looked at his teacher. "Poor Dianne."

Mr. Stones nodded. "Yes, poor Dianne. Think, too, of her family and all the others. A child is kidnapped, and waves spread out. Many people will suffer because of Dianne's disappearance. Even the kidnapper must be in agony, jumping in fear whenever a police car passes by, terrified of capture and the prison cell that awaits. Yes, many will suffer."

"We've got to get her back, sir!"

Mr. Stones' eyes stared at Tom from their dark sockets. "I know you're constantly reading those Hardy Boy mysteries, but don't get involved. Your father's an officer in an excellent police department. They'll find Dianne."

Tom nodded, but in his mind he thought, *Maybe they'll need some help.*

*   *   *

Inside the office of Mr. Nicholson, the principal, Tom sat on a wooden chair. The principal's arms and legs were very long, so he was secretly called "Bones". He stood at the window, watching a few snowflakes drift down from the white sky. The trees looked cold, dancing in the wind.

"Poor Dianne," Mr. Stones said quietly, cracking the knuckles of his big hands.

The school bell jangled, and feet thundered past the office.

The door opened, and in walked Officer Larson with Tom's father. Inspector Austen wore his police uniform, and carried his uniform cap. Just home from Mexico, his skin was brown from the sun. "I understand you've got some evidence for us," he said to Tom. "Well done."

Mr. Nicholson gestured at two chairs. "Sit down, please, gentlemen. Mr. Stones and I haven't yet heard Tom's evidence, but he assures us it's important."

"What happened, son?" Inspector Austen asked.

"Well, Dianne passed my patrol post after school yesterday."

"What time was that?" Officer Larson asked.

"Exactly 15:22. That's when she passes me every day."

Inspector Austen smiled. "You kept careful track of her movements, Tom?"

Tom blushed. "I don't know. I guess so."

"Carry on, son."

"Well, after Dianne went by, I, well..." Tom faltered to a stop. He would have to confess his mistake.

"Well, I left my post and followed Dianne. I know I shouldn't have, but I didn't think any more kids would be coming along."

Mr. Nicholson made a disapproving sound. He wrote something on a piece of paper, then waited for Tom to continue.

"I was close to Dianne when..." Tom paused, remembering the van. If only he had yelled *Don't get in!* "A small van stopped to give Dianne a ride."

"What?" Tom's father looked surprised. "Is that accurate, Tom?"

"Sure, Dad. That's what I saw."

"Excellent, excellent." Tom's father smiled. "That gives us a very important lead. Now, Tom, think carefully. What else can you tell us?"

Tom was delighted by his father's praise. He searched his memory. "Well, the driver said something to Dianne."

"Did you see the driver?" Officer Larson interrupted.

"No, I didn't." Tom hesitated. All this was embarrassing, but he couldn't think of his feelings during an investigation. "I, well, I didn't want Dianne to see me, so I couldn't get any closer."

"A shame," Officer Larson said quietly. "If only you had seen the driver."

"But I do have an important clue," Tom quickly added. "As the van drove away, I noticed two words on the rear doors."

"What were they?" Mr. Stones asked.

"Blind Driver."

Mr. Stones laughed, a sudden sound. "Blind Driver? Come now, Tom, are you certain? Or is this another of your jokes?"

"No, sir," Tom said, looking up at the man. "I'm sure of it."

"But how can a driver be blind? I don't mean to laugh, but surely you've made a mistake? After all, how can a blind person drive a van?"

Mr. Nicholson nodded his head. "I agree." He looked at Mr. Austen. "Tom has quite an imagination for an 11-year-old. It's very possible that he made a mistake."

"But I didn't!" Tom looked at his father. "I saw the words! They said Blind Driver."

Officer Larson shook his head. "I don't know, Inspector. He's your son, and he's got a detective office in his attic, but does that make him a reliable witness? The words don't make sense."

Mr. Austen's blue eyes glanced at him. "My son is very bright. I trust him."

Officer Larson turned to Tom. "What was the van's license number?"

"I don't know." Tom looked unhappily at his father. "I'm sorry, Dad, but I didn't notice the license. I didn't think Dianne was being kidnapped."

"I understand, son. Did you hear anything?"

"Just Dianne saying hello to the driver, and accepting a ride. She seemed to know him."

"Describe the driver," Officer Larson said.

"I couldn't see him."

"Then you're making an assumption. The driver could have been a woman."

"I guess you're right."

Officer Larson shook his head disapprovingly but Inspector Austen smiled. "You've given us some valuable evidence, Tom. Well done!"

"As for me," Officer Larson said, glancing at Mr. Nicholson, "I'd have been happy with a plate number. *That* would have been great."

Tom was suddenly angry. "At least I saw the van! At least I've given you a lead!" He stared at Officer Larson. "Why didn't you protect Dianne? That's your job. Why don't you go and find her, instead of being mean to me? I'm trying to help!"

Tom's father reached forward and patted Tom's knee. "All right, son, all right. Calm down. If you're going to be a detective, you need a tough hide. Lots of adults are stressed out, and they can get sarcastic." Inspector Austen stood up. "This has been very useful. Well done, Tom."

Mr. Nicholson cleared his throat. He picked up a metal letter opener and tapped it against the fingers of his hand. A chill passed over Tom. Whenever a student was in trouble, Mr. Nicholson fiddled with that letter opener.

The principal's black eyebrows wriggled as he cleared his throat again. "I'm concerned about your son, Inspector Austen."

"Yes?" Tom's father said.

"It's not his schoolwork, which is satisfactory." Mr. Nicholson paused. "But Tom and his friend Dietmar Oban are the school comedians. Their practical jokes do not amuse me. Recently, a rumor spread in the schoolground that I'd lost my job. The children cheered and burst into songs of celebration. I was not amused." Mr. Nicholson stared at the others. He wore small glasses with wire rims, and his thin hair was turning grey. Lines marked his eyes and mouth. "Tom has now confessed to breaking the rules for school patrol. He left his post."

"But..." Tom protested.

The principal held up his hand. "It is true that you provided valuable evidence, Tom. *But* you also broke the rules."

Tom dropped his eyes to the floor.

"Therefore," Mr. Nicholson said, "I must ask you to resign from the school patrol."

Tom's head snapped up. "No! That's not fair, Mr. Nicholson. I love being on the patrol!"

Mr. Austen put his hand on Tom's shoulder. "You must accept your punishment, son," he said. "Mr. Nicholson is right. I appreciate your evidence. Now, take your medicine like a man."

"Yes, Dad," Tom said quietly.

"Fine, fine." Mr. Nicholson stood up. "Turn in your patrol belt after school, Tom."

He left the principal's office squeezing back tears. The hallway was lined with art projects, a riot of color, but Tom's vision was too blurry to see anything.

"Tom!"

Feet hurried his way, and then Mr. Stones was beside him. "I'm sorry, Tom. I shouldn't have laughed. I can't picture a blind man driving, but perhaps there's an explanation. Do you forgive me?"

"Sure, sir."

"You must have seen those words." Mr. Stones smiled. "Good detectives don't make mistakes."

Tom felt better. "We'll get Dianne back, sir. Trust me on this."

Their classroom was strangely quiet. The kids stared at the floor, or whispered together. All eyes were on Tom and Mr. Stones as they came in the door. As Tom sat down, he looked at a pencil on Dianne's desk. Only yesterday her fingers had touched it.

"Any news?" Dietmar asked. His eyes were solemn.

"Nothing," Mr. Stones replied, "except for the brown van spotted by Tom." He looked around the room. "We're all thinking about Dianne today." His voice was hoarse and he seemed about to cry. "It's a tragedy for us all."

Art held up his hand. "Do you think she's disappeared forever, sir?"

Mr. Stones shook his head. "I think Dianne's been kidnapped for money. She'll be back safely, once a ransom is paid." He stared out the window. "The only question is: what about the kidnappers? Will they be captured?"

Tom nodded. "You bet, sir. They haven't got a chance."

Mr. Stones nodded solemnly. "Perhaps you're right."

*   *   *

Soon after, a poster appeared showing Dianne's face under the huge word MISSING. Her face looked at Tom from posters in stores, on lampposts, inside car windows, and on classroom doors at Queenston School.

Brittney Hayes raised her hand. "Sir, all this stuff scares me. I hear about Dianne all the time. I'm terrified someone's going to kidnap *me*."

The teacher nodded. "Lots of kids feel that way right now, because of Dianne. It takes courage to admit you're scared. Want my advice? Be cautious, know what you'd do in an emergency, and then enjoy life." He looked around the classroom. "You should all feel proud that you've been asked to help find Dianne."

"What if we don't find her?" Tom Bennett asked.

"Then you'll have tried, just like everyone else. The whole city is doing its best."

After school that day, Tom felt horrible. He no longer had his patrol belt, he no longer had his duties. Walking home alone, he stopped to talk with Pete Tyler. The school custodian was attaching posters to telephone poles on Kingsway.

"I feel so terrible," Pete said to Tom. "Dianne was the friendliest kid in the school. Her father had better pay a ransom, and fast, but maybe he won't."

"Why?" Tom asked.

"Because he's a cheapskate and a rat and a swindler. I hate him."

"Really?" Tom said. "How come?"

"It's none of your business, sonny. Now go away, and let me work."

5

On Saturday afternoon, Tom declined a shopping trip with his parents and Liz. Instead, he had a piece of chocolate cake and a glass of milk while he read *The Twisted Claw* (the pages dry again), and then he went upstairs to his office.

It was in the attic, under the sloping roof. On the door was a warning: KEEP OUT! THIS MEANS YOU. Tom opened the padlock, then checked a tiny slip of paper wedged in the door frame. It was still in place, so no intruder had attempted to open the door.

The walls were covered with the titles of every Hardy Boys mystery, plus posters showing the Morse code and semaphore symbols. There were also maps of Canada, Manitoba, and Winnipeg, a portrait of Sherlock Holmes and, most prized of all, police posters of the Ten Most Wanted Criminals in Canada.

Tom carefully studied the mug shots, refreshing in his memory their scars, the way some noses were bent, and the look of one man who seemed to have a glass eye. Tom knew that eventually he would recognize one of these criminals, make an arrest, and be a hero. He daydreamed for a minute, then got to work.

At his desk, Tom thought about the kidnapping. A ransom would be paid, or the kidnappers arrested, and then Dianne would come home. Meanwhile, would she be okay? Tom had always liked Dianne because she stood up for herself at school. No one put her down, and almost everyone liked her. She was kind, and fair, and she believed in herself. These qualities made her strong, so Tom figured she had a good chance of getting through the kidnapping safely.

Who was responsible? Tom made notes on the brown van, and then thought back. Only a week earlier, Red's pickup truck had almost struck Dianne. Could the kidnapping be linked to the mysterious meeting between Red and the man shrouded inside the ski mask? Now Tom was writing fast. Red and the shrouded man had arranged a meeting for four o'clock today "at the Golden Boy". He looked at his watch: *only two hours to go*.

*   *   *

Outside, winter was battering the city a final time. The snowflakes were big and wet, making branches sag and the streets slippery.

Downtown, the snow made driving difficult. Traffic crawled across a bridge over the Assiniboine River near the huge building where the Manitoba government held its meetings. On a dome far above was a golden statue of a boy holding a sheaf of wheat; a torch in his hand glowed through the falling snow.

Not far away were some grim streets. Business was bad here, and the people were unhappy. Some had gathered for coffee at a seedy place called the Golden Boy Café, named for the nearby statue. They sat at the counter, exchanging bad political news while chewing on tough doughnuts and sipping weak coffee.

The door opened, admitting the cold wind. A stranger with a briefcase in hand stood in the doorway. He was short, with slicked-back red hair and bulging cheeks. His eyebrows were as black as shoe polish, and he appeared to have a faint moustache. People might have thought he was a short salesperson taking a break from the cold, but secretly he was Tom Austen.

Removing his parka, Tom revealed a blazer, shirt, and tie. After sitting down in a booth, he allowed his blue eyes to travel around the room, memorizing everything. He turned toward a cracked mirror and critically studied the city slicker he saw reflected. Perhaps a touch too heavy on the shoepolish when disguising the eyes, but not a bad job. No one would suspect he was a kid.

A waitress appeared above, holding an order pad. "Yeah, kid? Whattya having?"

"Milk," Tom muttered, annoyed.

The waitress glanced up from the order pad. "What's the magic word?"

"Please," Tom added.

As she marched away, Tom studied a man at the counter, wondering if he could be Red in disguise. The waitress returned with some milk in an old glass. The cow juice was warm, but Tom decided not to complain. He swallowed some, then almost choked on pieces of cotton batten that washed out of his bulging cheeks.

Spluttering and coughing, Tom slammed down the glass and wiped his mouth. Everyone was staring, but Tom decided not to complain.

The clock above the juke box read 4:01 p.m. when Red came in the door and signaled to the waitress for a coffee. Minutes passed while he sat brooding at the counter, stirring the liquid with a spoon while staring moodily at the snow outside. Then his face brightened. Leaning forward, he watched a brown van stop across the street.

On the back were two words: *Blind Driver*.

Throwing a coin on the counter, Red headed for the door. The moment he was outside, Tom leapt into action. Fumbling for money, he pulled on his parka. Hurrying into the storm, he saw Red getting into the brown van. The driver was hidden from view, so Tom scurried across the street and moved closer to the van in a low crouch.

In the driver's outside mirror, he saw a face hidden inside a ski mask. The window was open.

Tom crept forward.

"I'm terrified," the driver moaned. "I live in agony, awaiting arrest. You forced me into this scheme, and now I'm doomed."

"Relax." Red's voice was thick with scorn. "I've got no sympathy. You're a spineless, crawling coward. In 30 minutes, I'll collect the ransom at the Countess, and you'll never see me again. So just..."

"Wait a minute!" The eyes of the shrouded man had spotted Tom. "There's a boy listening. I think I know him! He'll recognize me."

Red laughed. "Not with that ski mask you're wearing. Get out of here, and meet me at the Countess. I'll speak to the boy."

A door slammed, and the van pulled away. Red stood in the street—his eyes were mean. "So!" He stared at Tom. "The same kid from the school patrol. I warned you about being snoopy. *Now you're going to regret it.*"

Making two big fists, the man started walking toward Tom.

*   *   *

Tom ran, fast. Down the street he went, dodging past buses and slow-moving cars. Over his shoulder, he saw Red following. The man was a strong runner, and was close behind when Tom spotted the Greyhound terminal. With a final burst of energy, he raced inside. The bus station was crowded with travelers and suitcases, and buzzed with conversation. Close to Tom was a man in a peaked cap. On his uniform jacket were the words *Security Guard*.

"Help," Tom gasped, stopping beside the guard. "I've found Dianne Dorchester's kidnappers!"

The man's eyes widened. "*What*?"

"It's true," Tom exclaimed. He pointed at Red, coming into the terminal. "Arrest him!"

Red approached with a big smile on his face. "Is my son causing trouble again? He's such a prankster."

The security guard looked down at Tom. "This boy claims you kidnapped the missing girl."

Red's smile was very charming. "He loves playing detective. Look at that moustache he's penciled on, and the shoepolish on his eyebrows. Always in disguise! Don't you believe he's my son? His red hair's the same color as mine." Red grabbed Tom's arm. "Come on, son. I'm taking you home."

Tom slammed his foot down on Red's toes. The man yelled, and his grip loosened. Tearing free, Tom took off running. People stared as he raced between two buses, darted across an empty loading bay, and reached the street. Dropping into hiding behind a trash container, he looked at the terminal.

Through the windows he saw the men, still talking. Then Red hurried outside, jumped into a taxi, and was gone. Tom looked at his watch. He had ten minutes to reach the Countess.

*　　*　　*

The wind howled around Tom as he struggled from street to street until he reached the railway station. It was large, with pillars, and faced a parking lot.

In the middle of the lot was the Countess of Dufferin, one of the steam engines that first pulled trains across the prairies and high mountain passes all the way to Vancouver on the Pacific coast. Now the Countess was retired, and had become a favorite place for kids who liked to climb.

Tom stood by the parking lot, staring at the Countess. Someone was inside the engineer's cab. He could see a man in a dark overcoat and an expensive hat—it was Mr. Dorchester! Tom stared in amazement as Dianne's father climbed down the engine's ladder and dropped to the snow. Then he got into a car and drove away.

Out of a side street came the van with the man in the ski mask at the wheel. Red got out beside the Countess. Climbing the ladder, he disappeared inside the cab of the locomotive.

Tom remembered Mr. Stones saying, *When you need help, look for someone in a uniform, or a taxi driver who can radio the police.* Close by, a woman sat in her taxi in front of the station.

But the shortest route was straight past the Countess.

*　　　*　　　*

Gathering courage, Tom ran. Just as he dashed by the old steam engine, he saw Red above at the cab's door. Under the man's arm was a brown package.

Red spotted Tom. "Hey, you," he shouted. "You're that troublemaking kid. Stop!"

Tom didn't obey. Stumbling forward through the snow, he waved at the taxi driver. She rolled down her window. "What happened to your face? What's all that guck?"

"No time to explain," Tom cried. "Get the police here, please!"

"Will do," the woman replied, grabbing the microphone for her radio.

Tom looked back at the Countess. Red had scrambled down the ladder and now stood beside the locomotive, the package tucked safely under his arm. Somewhere in the distance, a siren wailed.

"The police are coming," Tom cried at the man. "Give up, now!"

Without a word, Red leapt into the van. Slipping and sliding, it left the parking lot. The taxi driver opened the passenger door, waved Tom inside, and they took off in pursuit. "We'll stop them," she smiled, stomping the accelerator, "I'm a champion at the wheel."

Rounding a corner, they raced into an industrial area with small businesses, used car lots, and gas stations. Ahead was the brown van, fighting its way through the storm. As the taxi moved closer, the van went out of control; whirling in a circle, it slammed into a snow bank.

Wheels spinning hopelessly, the van failed to break free. As Red jumped out to push, the taxi driver stopped and got out with Tom. Somewhere nearby, a siren howled closer. "The cops are coming," the driver shouted at Red. "Give up!"

Red grabbed the ransom package and took off running. At the same moment, the van broke free from the snow. Tires skidding, it fishtailed down the street and was gone.

The taxi driver and Tom went after Red. The man ran into an alley, but it was a dead end. Brick buildings loomed above, trapping Red. Clutching the ransom package, he stared at the taxi driver and Tom as they came closer.

"Give us the package," the driver said. "Surrender."

"Forget it, lady."

With a look of shock, Tom pointed over Red's shoulder. "Police dog! Look out!"

With a cry of fear, Red spun around. Tom threw himself against the man's legs, and knocked him down. The ransom package fell to the snow, and was grabbed by the taxi driver. She took off running, with Red in pursuit. As they reached the street, a police car came out of the storm and skidded to a stop.

Red reached inside his jacket. A revolver appeared in his hand. He waved it at Tom. "Back off, kid. Don't make me use this thing." Running to the police car, Red aimed the gun at the officer inside. "Out of this car," he yelled. "I need it more than you do."

Red fired shots at the taxi's front tires, taking it out of action. He jumped into the police car and it raced away down the street, leaving Tom alone with the police officer and the taxi driver. People were staring from the doors and windows of nearby businesses.

"I've got the ransom," the taxi driver said excitedly to Tom. "That was great, how you scared him in the alley by pretending to see a dog."

Tom beamed proudly. "I remembered the first time I saw Red. He was really scared of a dog."

The stolen police car was later recovered, but Red

escaped into hiding. Police raided his house and found evidence of his involvement in Dianne's kidnapping, but nothing that helped find the missing girl.

Things didn't look good for Dianne.

6

The next day, Tom decided to check out Dianne's house. He'd never seen it before, and was surprised at its size. The stone house stood alone in the middle of an enormous estate beside the river. All around the estate was a brick wall to keep out intruders.

A security guard stood by the wooden gate. With suspicious eyes, he watched Tom's approach. "Yeah, kid, what do you want?"

"Um..." Tom hadn't expected this kind of security. "Uh, any chance of a house tour?"

"Not a hope."

"But I'm a friend of Dianne's. We go to Queenston School together."

"Her family's too upset to see anyone."

Tom looked across the vast lawn at the house. Nothing moved behind the windows. "Any idea who's involved in the kidnapping?" he asked the guard.

"Nope."

The man went inside a small security office and poured himself a coffee. Tom moved closer, memorizing every detail of the small office. Windows faced the gate and looked over the estate; he saw a small desk and two chairs, a filing cabinet and a telephone.

"Hey," Tom suddenly exclaimed, "there's our school newspaper! I'm one of the editors."

The guard picked up the paper. "Yeah, another guard left this here. His kid is Elizabeth Whitman—she took these pictures of the school staff. He's real proud of her."

"Elizabeth's my friend, too."

The man smiled. "Hey, you're doing okay for girlfriends." He pointed at one of the pictures. "See this guy? I met him a few months ago when he tried to get a job here, as a security guard. He claimed to be sick of working at Queenston School, but I kind of wondered why. Guarding this gate can get pretty boring."

Tom didn't reply because his mouth was hanging open in surprise. The man who'd tried for a job at the Dorchester estate was Pete Tyler, the school custodian.

"Yeah," the security guard continued, "he almost got a job, but then Mr. Dorchester found out about his criminal record."

*   *   *

At school the next day, Tom discussed the case with his friend Stephen Xu as they went into their classroom, where a huge banner proclaimed *Welcome to Kids Day!* It was strung above the board in Tom's classroom. Mr. Stones had made a big effort, drawing a portrait of each student. These filled the walls, and streamers hung above.

"Life must continue," he said, when everyone was seated. "We all miss Dianne terribly, but I decided to have Kids Day despite her disappearance. We all need to cheer up." He tried to smile. "Especially me."

Stephen held up his hand. "Sir, I've got a suggestion. When Dianne returns, let's have Kids Day, Part Two. That'll be a real celebration!"

"Great idea," Dietmar said. "That'll give us an extra holiday."

Other students praised Stephen's suggestion, and then he held up his hand again. "Mr. Stones, here's another idea. When the kidnappers go on trial, let's have a field trip to the courtroom. We can watch the judge sentence them to prison."

Mr. Stones sighed. "I'm sure you're right, Stephen. They will certainly end up behind bars. That makes me sad."

"Why, sir?"

"Not everyone *wants* to be a criminal, you know. Some people get dragged into crime because they have no money, others because they have no hopes or dreams for the future. Our world offers them nothing." His eyes were fierce under the thick brows. "Still others are forced into crime at the point of a gun. Think of a poor man like that, driven into crime. What misery does he feel? Does he think about the prison bars—how cold they will feel to his hands? Does he picture his wife and children, visiting through a wire fence at the prison? What are that poor man's thoughts? What are his regrets?"

The room was silent, all eyes on Mr. Stones.

He forced himself to smile. "That's my thought for the day. A long one, I admit! Now, let's have some fun." After closing the blinds against the sun, he looked at Amardeep Dhaliwal. "Tell us a joke, Amardeep."

The friendly student grinned. "What do you get when you cross an elephant with a horse? A pony with big feet."

As everyone laughed, Mr. Stones pulled some papers from his pocket including some old receipts from *Pizza Perfect* and a few other restaurants. "Ah, here's what I want! I've written an Honor Roll of your accomplishments. Every one of you is a winner, I'm pleased to say. You'll receive a Certificate of Achievement." He looked at Elizabeth Whitman. "You're first, Elizabeth. Recently I boarded a crowded bus, and saw you giving up your seat to someone. Well done!"

Smiling shyly, she received her certificate. As the honors continued for other students, Mr. Nicholson appeared in the doorway. With him was a stranger.

"Tom Austen," the principal said. "This man's from the newspaper. He wants to interview you about the kidnapping."

"Wow!" Tom glowed. "You bet—for sure!"

The man shook hands. "The name's Byron Xavier Lewis. Call me B.X., everyone does." Thin and short, he wore a crumpled shirt and trousers. His collar was open at the neck, showing an Adam's apple that moved when he spoke. "So, you're the hero who almost captured the kidnappers." B.X. had pale grey eyes that flicked from Tom to Mr. Stones to Mr. Nicholson, then back to Tom. "Tell me how you did it."

"Sure," Tom said, "but where's your notebook?"

"Huh?"

"How will you remember what I say for your newspaper article?"

"Oh!" B.X. swallowed. Digging around in his pockets, he pulled out a crumpled restaurant napkin. "This'll do."

"Need a pen?" Mr. Stones asked, offering one.

B.X. gave the teacher a curt nod. "Thanks, fella." He looked at Tom. "So, how many kidnappers were there?"

"Two."

"Did you identify them?"

"One, the guy named Red. The police raided his place, but he's gone into hiding. He lived next door to a deserted house, and they think he used it for secret meetings. I saw one with my own eyes."

B.X. wasn't writing anything down, he was just watching Tom. "What do you mean?"

"The night before the kidnapping, I was hiding in the attic. I saw Red with another man."

"My goodness!" Mr. Stones leaned across his desk. "Tom, is that true? That's important information."

B.X. studied Tom. "Did you recognize the other man?"

"No, because he was disguised in a ski mask." Watching B.X.'s face, he saw the worry lines relax. The man hadn't written a word since the interview began. Tom looked at Mr. Stones. "Okay to leave the room, sir? I'm not feeling well, too much lemonade I guess. I'll phone my Mom for a ride home."

Tom hurried down the hallway. At the principal's office, he borrowed a phone book, then called the newspaper. "Hello," he said. "May I please speak to a reporter named Byron Xavier Lewis?" There was a silence, during which the school secretary studied Tom's face. Then he said thanks, and hung up. "The newspaper's never heard of that man," he told her.

B.X. appeared in the doorway with Mr. Nicholson. Both of them looked upset. "You didn't finish the interview," B.X. said. "I've got some more questions."

"You're not a reporter," Tom told him. "You're just trying to get information from me. How come?"

B.X. turned to the principal. "Thanks for your help," he said. "I'm on my way." Quickly he went into the pale sunshine of early spring, and walked away.

"Sir," Tom said urgently to the principal. "Arrest that guy! He's a fake reporter."

Crossing his arms, Mr. Nicholson gazed down at Tom. "Another gag, young Mr. Austen? Another not-very-funny prank?"

"Phone the newspaper yourself, sir! It's true!"

"In your classroom, you said you were sick. Weren't you going to phone your mother for a ride?"

"Sure, but..."

"You lied, Tom. Go to your classroom, immediately. I'll deal with you later."

Head hanging, Tom walked mournfully along the hallway. Pausing at the school's side door, he looked outside. The fake reporter named Byron Xavier Lewis was waiting at a bus stop.

"Hey, Austen!" Dietmar Oban appeared beside Tom. "What's going on? Mr. Stones wants to know how sick you are. I told him you should be in an institution. He sent me looking for you."

Grabbing Dietmar by the arm, Tom pushed open the door. The air was cool outside. "I need some help, Oban."

"Forget it!"

"You like Elizabeth Whitman, right?"

"Maybe."

"Tell you what, Oban. I'll write you some poetry to give her. She'll fall in love for sure."

"What's the price?"

"A short bus ride." Tom dragged Dietmar across the school yard. "Hurry up, I see a bus coming now."

"This is insanity, Austen! We'll be in deep trouble at the school."

"We've got no choice. Come on, climb aboard."

Tom forced Dietmar into the bus. As it lurched away from the curb, he saw B.X. watching them from the back seat. The other passengers were a mother and her baby, and a white-haired man gripping a cane. "They could be his accomplices," Tom whispered to Dietmar as they sat down at the front. "Act innocent."

"What's going on?" Dietmar demanded.

"That guy isn't a reporter. He was trying to find out if I recognized the second kidnapper. He must be part of their gang. If we follow him, we may find where Dianne's hidden."

The bus swung hard around a corner, pitching the boys forward. Tom stared at the driver, wondering if he was also involved. He began to sweat—maybe they'd blundered into maximum danger.

Dietmar looked at him. "I just thought of something. How can we follow that guy when he's already seen us?"

"I'll think of something," Tom promised. "Trust me."

"That poetry better be good, Austen."

Tom got out his notebook. "One thing I've learned today," he told Dietmar as he made notes on the case. "There are at least three guys in the kidnap ring. Red and B.X., plus the man in the ski mask."

"Maybe that was B.X.," Dietmar suggested.

"No, he's far too short."

"Why don't you phone the cops?"

"I will, the minute B.X. leads us to the kidnappers' hiding place. If he gets scared, and escapes, Dianne won't be found."

Slowly, the bus made its way downtown. Outside, yards were brown after the long winter and snow still lingered in shady places. As the bus crossed a bridge over the Assiniboine, the boys gasped. "Look at the river!" Dietmar exclaimed. "It's a raging torrent."

The brown water surged past. Swollen by melting snow, it had climbed the river banks almost to the bridge. High above the flood-threatened city, the Golden Boy held his torch aloft. Tom and Dietmar watched him through the window, then the bus continued downtown past department stores and businesses and churches with onion-shaped domes. Other people left and entered, but B.X. remained on board. His eyes never left the boys.

*   *   *

Finally, B.X. left the bus in an industrial area. There were warehouses along the street, and equipment yards surrounded by chain-link fences.

As the bus drove away, B.X. gave the boys a dirty look. "You two following me?"

Tom stared at him. "Why'd you question me at the school? You're a kidnapper, not a reporter."

"Rubbish," the man scoffed. "Now beat it, both of you."

"Or you'll call the cops?" Tom said. "I doubt it."

"You're right," the man said, making a fist, "but I'll use this on your front teeth."

Dietmar gulped. "Come on, Austen. Let's go home."

Tom nodded. "Okay, but we'll have to walk. I'm out of bus fare."

As the boys went down the street, Tom used a tiny pocket mirror to watch B.X. The man stared after them, then hurried toward a side street and was gone. "Let's follow him," Tom said urgently, running toward the street. "Come on, Oban!"

"Forget it, Austen."

"I'll write you *five* poems."

"No deal."

"But that guy could lead us to Dianne!"

"Okay, Austen, but I don't like this."

"Nothing will happen, and we've got to learn where Dianne's a prisoner."

Scurrying between parked cars, the boys followed B.X. along a dusty street until he reached a furniture warehouse where large banners read *Closed Due to Bankruptcy*. After glancing up and down the street, B.X. went inside.

"Let's call the cops," Dietmar said.

"First, let's make sure Dianne's in that warehouse. It'll only take a minute."

"This feels like quicksand," Dietmar said. "I keep getting deeper and deeper, and I never wanted to be here anyway."

"You'll be famous, Oban. Isn't that important to you?"

"Not in the slightest."

Tom shook his head. "Sometimes you're so weird, Oban. All I want from life is my picture in the newspaper."

"It'll probably happen, but you'll have a number on your chest and be wearing a striped prison suit."

"Funny, funny." Tom raised a warning hand. "Now, pipe down, Oban. We're going into that warehouse."

The boys raced across a litter-filled yard and tried the door. "It's open," Tom whispered. "Come on." Passing along a short hallway, they entered the furniture warehouse. Pale light came through dirty windows, showing a roof far above. Some furniture was stored on enormous shelves, but most was displayed on the big floor. They could see sofas and tables and beds and several piles of mattresses.

At the far end of the warehouse was a steel staircase, rising to the floor above. Up there was a small office, where a light glowed through an open door.

"Look," Tom said, "there's B.X. Let's get closer."

"Hold it, Austen. My nose is vibrating—I think I'm allergic to something in here. I'd better wait outside."

"You've got an allergy?" Tom said with heavy sarcasm. "Since when?"

"It's true, Austen! I'm going to sneeze, for sure."

"Stick with me," he said, squeezing Dietmar's arm. "We're almost finished."

"That's what I'm afraid of."

Reaching the steel staircase, they crept up. Dust danced in the light from the office, where B.X. stood in the doorway and Red sat behind a desk. "Honest, boss," B.X. whined, "I tried. Everyone at the school believed I was a reporter."

"Except the kid himself," Red snarled. "But at least you learned he didn't recognize my man in the ski mask. That's good news. It was worth taking a risk by sending you as a fake reporter."

"I did a good job, boss."

"Did you use a fake name at the school?"

"No. Was I supposed to?"

"Of course, you fool!"

"Sorry, boss."

"Ah, forget it. Your name isn't in the phone book, so the cops can't track you down."

"Something I can't figure, boss. Why'd you need another person to help us?"

"Like I told you before, nitwit, we needed someone Dianne knew to drive the van. I was pretty sure I could find a helper at that school."

Tom climbed higher up the stairs, pulling Dietmar along. The office looked down at the display floor, far below. The displays could also be watched from a steel catwalk that connected to the office. Trying for a better look at the two men, Tom led Dietmar onto the catwalk.

"I'm terrified of heights," Dietmar moaned. "Get me out of here."

"Don't look down. That's always a mistake."

Tom signaled for quiet. Now he had a clear view of Red, who was smoking a cigar behind the desk. "I've made a decision," the man told B.X. "We're going to leave town. Just for a while, until the pressure lets up. Then we'll try again for a ransom payment."

"Sounds good," B.X. said.

"We're moving to our hideout in Ontario. I'll take 2014 and you drive there in the pickup truck. You know where to meet me."

"What about the Dorchester brat?"

"We can't take a chance on moving her. Not with posters of her face all over town."

"Your man in the ski mask will keep feeding her?"

"He'd better." Red stubbed out the cigar. "Let's get going."

As the man stood up, Tom realized they were now

trapped on the catwalk—it was impossible to reach the stairs without being seen. Motioning to Dietmar, he led him farther out the catwalk. Far below, the furniture was only dim shapes in the faint light.

"Don't make a sound, Oban," he whispered.

Dietmar's only response was a moan.

The men's footsteps echoed as they descended the metal stairs. In a corner of the warehouse, Red pulled a tarpaulin to one side. Hidden behind it were two vehicles. "There's Red's pickup truck," Tom whispered to Dietmar, "and there's the brown van. Now I understand why it says *Blind Driver* on the back. It's for delivering blinds and other furniture."

Red rolled open a big outside door, and B.X. drove away in the pickup truck. Then, moments later, Dietmar sneezed. The sound blasted through the warehouse, echoing between the walls. As Tom stared at him, Dietmar gestured with his hands. "Sorry! But I warned you."

Red headed for the stairs, moving fast. "You little meddlers," he shouted. "I'm going to arrange an accident for you. It's a long fall from that catwalk to the display floor."

Tom looked for another escape route, but they were trapped. Dietmar's eyes were huge with fear. "Help," he groaned. "Do something!"

Tom pointed down at the piles of mattresses. "Let's jump. It's our only chance."

"Jump? You've got to be kidding!"

"You want to get thrown off by Red? Come on, move!"

"No more investigations, Austen. Never!" Dietmar climbed on the catwalk railing, groaned once, and jumped.

Tom looked at Red. He had reached the catwalk and was moving fast. "I'll get you, kid," he snarled.

Tom's stomach clenched with fear as he jumped. His heart rose into his throat, then he slammed into the mattresses.

"Come on, Dietmar," he yelled, rolling off them, "run!"

The boys dashed into the street. Moments later, the brown van raced away with Red behind the wheel. "Find a phone," Tom told Dietmar. "Call the police!"

"What will you do?"

"I've got a hunch where Red's gone. I'm going to check it out, and call the police if I'm right."

"I can go now?"

"You bet, Oban. Thanks for your help."

"Remember just one thing, Austen. *Never again*."

7

Before long, Tom reached the railway station. He looked at the Countess of Dufferin, remembering the chase after Red and wondering how the man always escaped. He was a slippery character, for sure.

Passing between enormous pillars, Tom entered the station. Sunshine flowed through windows high above, warming the crowds waiting for a train's departure. Some people cried in each other's arms while luggage handlers rushed by with suitcases.

At the *Train Departures* notice board, Tom's eyes lit up. As he'd thought, there was a train with the number 2014 departing now. And Red had spoken of leaving town on the 2014!

Tom looked for a phone booth to call his father at

the police station. People stood in every one, talking to friends and relatives. Meanwhile, the station slowly emptied as people boarded 2014 and loudspeakers warned it was about to leave the station.

The people still gabbed on the phones! Tom realized he would have to board the train and alert the conductor to arrest Red. He ran out of the station to the corner, went through an underpass, and reached the railway yards.

The tracks spread out like metal spaghetti in every direction. Yard engines shunted back and forth while freight cars crashed together, creating an exciting scene, but one that Tom had no time to stop and enjoy.

He looked across the yard. Standing quietly in the midst of all the motion was a long string of passenger cars, steam drizzling from couplings and hidden pipes. At the head of the cars was a big diesel engine, ready to take the train on its journey east.

Tom stumbled on the wooden ties as he ran across the yard, anxiously hoping the engine wouldn't move. A woman looked up from her work and stared at Tom as he ran past, his breath heaving in and out. A whistle on the engine shrieked and Tom ran faster.

He rounded the end of the train and pulled his tired body up onto the station platform. Another blast from the whistle. He looked along the train and saw that the porters had already climbed inside and closed the doors; the only person left on the platform was a distant conductor waving his arm toward the engine.

It seemed too late, but Tom found the energy to make his legs carry him toward a sleeping car where the top half of the door was open. A young woman leaned out, watching Tom.

"Please," Tom gasped, looking up at the woman. "Please, open the door."

"What did you say?" she shouted above the hissing of steam from couplings.

"Open the door," Tom yelled, pointing to the handle. "My mother is sick!"

A puzzled frown appeared on the woman's face, and she looked toward the end of the train as if expecting a sick mother to appear in a wheelchair.

"Open the door!" Tom repeated.

This time the woman seemed to understand; she reached for the handle, took a few seconds figuring out how it worked, then pulled the door open. But a steel platform still lay across the steps, preventing Tom from boarding the train.

"The platform!" Tom yelled, pointing at a metal catch that held the steel plate in place. "Push that catch with your foot!"

The woman looked down at the catch, puzzled once again. The train lurched as the big engine started forward.

"KICK THAT CATCH," Tom shrieked, dancing from one foot to the other. He started to run beside the train as it rolled forward, pointing desperately at the catch. The woman kicked feebly at it, then tried again and the steel plate came free, rising up out of Tom's way. He jumped onto the bottom step and grabbed a railing, unable to speak as the train rattled out of the station.

"Are you all right?" the young woman asked anxiously.

Tom nodded, still holding tightly to the railing.

"Where is your mother? Did she miss the train?"

Tom shook his head, more interested in catching his breath than lying to the woman. Besides, in the fight against crime, no one could be trusted. "My mother will be fine," he panted, "just fine."

"Where is she? Does she need help?"

"No, thanks." Climbing up the steps, Tom slammed the steel plate back into place and closed the door. "Thanks for helping me."

Tom gifted the woman with a bright smile as he pushed open the door of the car. He would have to find the conductor and alert him.

The train swayed back and forth as it left the yards and began to pick up speed. Tom looked into the back yards of some old houses, and then was startled by a rumbling sound as the train rolled onto a steel trestle. He looked down at the deep brown waters of the Red River surging past under the trestle, and felt suddenly afraid of the rising flood waters.

The clatter of the couplings was loud in Tom's ears as he crossed the shaking metal plates that connected to the next car. Somewhere, behind a closed door, a baby was crying. Tom moved slowly through the train, looking carefully at the passengers, aware that Red could be in disguise. He reached the end of the car, crossed more shaking metal plates, and entered another car.

Faintly, in the distance, the train's whistle sounded. Tom looked out the window as they flashed through a tiny town and roared back onto the open prairie. Green buds showed on trees gathered together near water, and spring sunshine warmed the fields.

No crying baby in this car. Tom hurried along the aisle, receiving some hostile looks from the faces he was examining. One man was hidden behind a newspaper he was reading and Tom hesitated, not wanting to waste time, but not wanting to miss any faces. How to get a look? The problem was solved by the man, who lowered the paper. It was Red.

"Oh!" Tom said, shocked. He could feel the blood draining away from his face as he stared at Red's jacket—he could see the outline of a shoulder holster!

Tom began to back away, almost tripping as his feet tangled together.

"Just a minute," Red said sharply. He put down his newspaper and seemed to reach toward his jacket.

"Don't shoot," Tom cried. "The police have the train surrounded!"

A strange look passed across Red's face. He tried to grab Tom but his hand clutched thin air. People watched in astonishment as Tom dashed to the end of the car, where a door marked *Toilet* stood half open. Fear shaking his body, he rushed inside and slammed the door shut.

Red's feet crashed to a stop outside the door. Tom turned the lock.

"Open up!" Red's voice called.

Tom leaned against the door, his eyes filled with terror as he watched the handle moving back and forth. He looked around the tiny washroom for a means of escape, but there was nothing.

"What's the problem, sir?" a voice outside said.

"Nothing," Red replied. A pause, then he added, "My son has locked himself in the washroom. Can you open the door?"

"I can," the conductor replied, "but why should I?"

"He's got my razor blades. He's a hysterical boy, and I'm afraid he'll cut himself real bad."

Silence. Tom could picture the conductor trying to decide if Red was telling the truth.

"All right," the conductor said, "we'd better get him out of there."

A scraping sound of metal against metal as a key turned in the lock. Reaching inside, Red grabbed Tom.

"Come here, son." Red tried to sound like a friendly father, but his blue eyes were cold and mean as he yanked Tom out of the washroom.

"Where's the razor?" the conductor asked.

"There isn't one," Tom shouted. "This man's a kidnapper!"

Red slammed his hand over Tom's mouth but Tom bit him, hard. With a shout of pain, Red released his grip. But then he pulled a gun from his shoulder holster.

"Don't move, kid." He aimed the gun at a man sitting in one of the seats. "Try anything, and you're a dead turkey."

"I didn't..." the man protested.

"Don't interrupt!" Red locked a powerful hand on Tom's arm. "You must have sawdust for brains, kiddo. How can the police surround a moving train?"

"I don't know," Tom muttered. He looked around

for help, but the people in the car looked too afraid to move, and one man was even crying. Fear had changed their faces, making them look like trapped animals.

"What are you going to do?" Tom asked Red, trying not to sound afraid.

But the man ignored him. Glancing at his watch, he motioned with his gun along the car. "Get going," he said to the conductor, giving Tom's arm a rough tug. "You too, kiddo."

They started forward, the conductor in front with the pistol pointed at his head, Tom at Red's side.

"Anyone moves," Red shouted, "and the conductor qualifies for a nice funeral."

The crying man huddled in his seat as they approached. Red laughed. "Must be a cop."

The words made Tom furious. "You think the police are so stupid? They're going to ambush your gang. The baggage car is full of police, with guns and everything."

Red only laughed harder, and pushed Tom forward with the conductor. Between cars, surrounded by the crashing noise of the couplings, Tom grabbed his stomach.

"Oh," he groaned, "oh, I'm sick."

"Come on, keep moving," Red said angrily.

"I can't," Tom moaned, leaning forward and clutching his stomach tighter.

"What is it?" Red said, stopping to look at Tom.

As the man's grip loosened on his arm, Tom tore himself free. Before Red could move, he grabbed the emergency cord and pulled hard.

"You little fool!" Red shouted.

But it was too late to change anything. Steel wheels screeched against steel tracks as the brakes slammed on. Shuddering and bucking, the train came to a grinding halt in the middle of the prairie.

8

After the immense noise of the moving train, the silence filled Tom's ears. He stared at Red, waiting for the man to do something terrible, but the anger passed quickly from his blue eyes.

"Come here, kiddo." Gripping Tom's arm, Red turned to the conductor. "Open that door, Pops."

"Yes, sir. Don't shoot, sir."

After pulling open the door, the conductor kicked the catch to free the steel plate across the steps.

"Lie down and count to 50," Red barked.

"Yes, sir." The conductor lay down on his stomach. "One, two, three..."

"Let's go," Red ordered Tom. They went down the steps and jumped to the gravel beside the tracks.

"What's going on?" a man's voice yelled.

The porter in the next sleeping car had left the train and was looking their way. A cloud of steam hid him for a second, and when he reappeared his eyes were popping as he stared at Red's gun.

"Get back in the train!" Red shouted.

"Sure thing, sure thing," the man said, racing up the steps. The door of his car closed with a slam.

Another porter had climbed out far along at the head of the train, his white coat a distant blur in the sunshine. A few other people leaned out from the doors between the cars, but no one was coming to help Tom.

"This way," Red said, pulling him toward the end of the train. Faces looked down from the windows as they passed, feet grinding on the gravel.

"Faster." Red began to run, his hand holding firmly to Tom. They reached the end of the train and stopped, looking at the emptiness that stretched under billowing clouds to the distant horizon. Dust rose from the wheels of a car coming toward them along a dirt road.

"Flag him down," Red ordered.

Tom waved both arms. The driver, who had been staring at the train stopped in the middle of nowhere, braked beside Tom and Red.

"Hi!" he said, a friendly grin on his chubby face. He had a pimply nose, and wore a hat too small for his head. "What's going on?"

Red pointed the revolver at the man's head. "I don't know what's going on, Jumbo, but this is going off unless you give us a ride."

The grin melted off the chubby face. "I've got a wife and kids," the man said. "Don't shoot me."

"You want them to have a father tomorrow, you do what I say."

"Yes, sir."

Keeping his gun aimed at the driver, Red pulled Tom around the car to the passenger door. They climbed in beside the fat man.

"Let's go," Red said, slamming the door.

"Yes, sir."

The driver's nervous foot jumped off the clutch and the car leapt forward, rocks and dirt shooting from the wheels. "Sorry," the driver shouted above the noise, his hands fighting the steering wheel as they bounced along the road and left the train behind.

"Where to, sir?" the driver asked.

"Ontario."

"What!?"

"You heard me, Jumbo. Ontario, and don't spare the horsepower."

"But I'm a salesman. I've got clients to see today."

Red laughed. "My brother is an undertaker. You want to be his client?"

"No, sir," the fat man said. "No, sir."

"Follow back roads. The cops may set up roadblocks on the highway."

Sitting between the driver and Red, Tom looked at the black revolver and wondered if Red would really use it. He seemed to make a lot of threats, but no one was a dead turkey yet. Still, Tom didn't think it would be good for his health to call Red's bluff. At least, not yet.

A large checkerboard sign appeared ahead. Turning onto a paved road, the car picked up speed as it headed across the flat land. Tom saw horses grazing in a field, their tails lazily twitching, but no other sign of life. As flies and bugs splattered against the windshield, he tried to think of an escape plan. The fuel gauge registered full, meaning there wouldn't be a chance to make a break during a pit stop. He looked up at the driver, wondering if an escape plan was forming in the man's head.

"What do you sell?" Tom asked the driver.

"Ladies' underwear," the fat man muttered.

As Red roared with laughter, the driver's chubby face went red. Tom was silent, unable to think of another question.

"Boy, oh, boy," Red chuckled, "ladies' underwear."

A boy walking along the side of the road with a yellow dog looked at Tom as they passed. Would he alert the police? Not much chance, since he wouldn't know Tom had been kidnapped.

Kidnapped! Tom suddenly realized what had happened—this was just like a Hardy Boys mystery, but he was sure Dianne wouldn't think kidnapping was an adventure. Tom looked up at Red.

"Why did you kidnap Dianne?" he said, watching his face closely.

Red glanced at Tom. "Button your lip, kiddo."

Tom was silent—obviously, Red could stand up to ruthless questioning. He tried to remember how Frank and Joe Hardy grilled criminals, but the books seemed like distant, faded memories.

The car tires hummed against the pavement as they rolled steadily onward, watching the land change from flat fields to bush and rock. After they'd passed a sign welcoming them to Ontario, Tom's stomach began to rumble.

"I'm hungry," he said.

"Aren't we all," Red murmured.

"Can't we stop for a milkshake?"

"Keep your shirt on, kiddo," Red said. "I'll fry up some fish later tonight."

"But I want to eat now," Tom insisted.

"You want a mouthful of lead?"

Tom didn't answer, still not certain if Red was bluffing with his gun. The sky above the prairie turned scarlet, streaked by black clouds. A single ray of the setting sun lit the earth. Tom saw more horses in a field.

"Are they wild?" he asked.

Jumbo shook his head. "Farmers own them. What a life, eh, out in the open with nothing to do but run wild and free."

Red glanced at him. "Hey, Jumbo, you're a poet, not a salesman. Why aren't you out there, writing?"

He shrugged his sloping shoulders. "I never took a chance in life. It's too late now to start over."

Red snorted. "I figure you only get one turn. Make it count, that's what I say."

Tom held up his hand. "Sorry, but I've *gotta* find a bathroom soon."

Red looked at him suspiciously. "Are you planning an escape? If so, think again. That's the only warning you get."

He motioned at Jumbo with his hand. "I see a campground ahead. Pull off there."

By now, Jumbo had the headlights on. The yellow beams spotted the campground. It had dirt roads, a few trees, some wooden picnic tables, and a central building with showers and washrooms. To Tom's dismay, no one was around to help.

Slowly, he got out of the car. As Red pushed him toward the washroom, Tom stumbled and then fell.

"My ankle," he cried. "You made me twist it!"

Red leaned forward to examine Tom's ankle. As he did, Tom grabbed some dirt and flung it into Red's face. Crying out, the man clawed at his eyes with both hands.

Tom ran toward the car. "Start the engine," he yelled at Jumbo, "let's get out of here!"

"You bet," the man shouted. The engine turned over, then died. Jumbo leaned over the wheel, desperately working the starter while his eyes watched Red wiping his face. "I've flooded the engine," Jumbo yelled as Tom reached the car. "It won't start!"

"Come on," Tom cried to the man, "let's use the horses!" Running toward a nearby field, he climbed to the top of the fence. It was now getting really dark, but he could see the horses.

Jumbo reached the fence, panting from the run, and began to climb. "I'm out of shape," he gasped, "please help me."

Reaching down, Tom helped the man over the fence and they hurried across the field. The horses stamped their feet nervously as Tom approached making soothing noises. Jumbo was just behind, but there was no sign of Red in the darkness.

Tom pulled himself onto one of the bare backs. The horse was warm to his touch. In the distance Red appeared, climbing over the fence. "Hurry, mister," Tom urged. "Get on that horse, and let's go!"

"I can't," the man moaned. "That thing's too high. I can't climb on it." Jumbo looked at Red. He was moving slowly, still wiping at his eyes, but he was coming their way. "Go ahead, kid, ride for safety! I'll be okay."

"No, I can't do that," Tom replied, sliding off the horse. "We'll make a break for it together."

Reaching a fence, Tom whistled in astonishment. "Here's a bicycle! It must belong to the farmer's kid."

"Are the tires inflated okay?"

"You bet," Tom said. "Hurry, we can ride double."

Jumbo shook his head. His entire body was trembling with fear. "I've tried that with my kids, and it doesn't work. My stomach's too big. Go ahead, ride out of here and find the police."

"No," Tom said, "you take the bike."

Jumbo stared fearfully at Red, who was coming their way. "I, I..."

"Take it," Tom urged. The man's fear made him sad. "Go on, you've got a wife and kids. What if they never see you again? Ride out of here, fast!"

"You're right," Jumbo mumbled, climbing on the bike, "they need me." The bicycle lurched forward under his big feet, then began to gather speed. Jumbo disappeared into the darkness, moving fast.

Tom ran in the opposite direction, following the fence. The ground was uneven for a while, then became smoother. Ahead, Tom saw the dim outline of picnic benches and a small building. Somehow he'd found his way back to the campground, where he'd seen a pay phone.

Tom crept through the darkness toward the building. The phone was attached to the outside wall. As Tom picked it up he looked at the surrounding night. It was absolutely silent, and he couldn't see anything.

"*Operator*," a voice said on the phone. "*What number, please*?"

"Thank goodness," Tom exclaimed. "Listen, operator, I'm in big trouble!"

"*Yes*?"

Tom heard a footstep, somewhere behind. He whirled around, staring at the dark air. Nothing could be seen. Still he stared, then raised the phone to his ear. "Sorry, operator, I thought that..." Stopping, Tom looked at the phone in his hand. It had gone dead.

Again he heard a sound, and this time saw Red. The man had pulled out the telephone wire and was twirling it in one hand. In the other, he held the gun. It was pointed straight at Tom.

*   *   *

"You're some kid."

Red was with Tom in the salesman's car. "You've got a lot of courage, I'll say that, but I'm starting to get upset." He looked at Tom. "We're driving to Lake of the Woods. It's mighty big, and mighty deep. One more trick, and I'll deep-six you in the lake. Know what that means?"

Tom gulped, and nodded.

Without another word, Red headed for the road and they continued their journey into the night. At last, two reflectors appeared ahead in the dark, shining in the headlights like the eyes of a cat. As they came closer, Tom saw the reflectors were on the back of a pickup truck parked beside the highway. B.X. was at the wheel.

Red pulled the salesman's car off the road, left the keys inside, and ran with Tom to the pickup.

"Hey," B.X. demanded as they climbed into the front seat. "What happened to you? I waited at the Junction, but 2014 never showed up. So I came here to wait, like we agreed."

"Tell you later, B.X. Let's get going."

Soon the pickup was flying down the highway, much faster than the salesman had managed with his car. Tom watched anxiously as the speedometer needle climbed, afraid a tire would blow and they'd overturn in a ditch.

"Take it easy, B.X.," Red said. "I want to die of old age."

Their speed dropped slightly. The trip continued in silence until the pickup abruptly turned onto a gravel surface. The trees at the side of the road seemed thicker as they followed the road up and around several hills.

"Can you drive a car, kiddo?"

"Not yet," Tom replied.

"What a shame. I could use a new driver. B.X. is too fast."

"Yeah!"

Red laughed, and B.X.'s mouth turned down at the corners. "What'll we do with this kid?" he asked. "Ransom him for money?"

"Nah. His family's not rich. Maybe I'll just use him for target practice."

Tom didn't let his face show anything. He was sure now that Red was bluffing with that gun, so he wasn't afraid of becoming a target.

"Nerves of steel, huh?" Lifting the gun, Red put the cold muzzle against Tom's temple. The hammer of the gun clicked. Tom closed his eyes and forced himself to pretend that he was back in school, adding up numbers in math. When he opened his eyes, Red had lowered the gun.

"Here we are," B.X. said.

As they got out, he switched on a flashlight. Holding tight to Tom, Red followed B.X. along a dirt path. Tom heard water swishing, and the soft slap of waves, then saw the flashlight beam hit a powerful speedboat.

"Hey," he said, unable to keep his excitement from showing. "Is that your boat?"

Laughing, Red gave B.X. a poke on the arm. "Keep moving."

The flashlight beam stopped on an old rowboat with an outboard motor clamped to the back. Tom stepped down into the boat, staggering as it rocked back and forth. "Give the engine a kick and let's get going," Red ordered B.X.

Tom saw the brilliance of a thousand stars above the lake. The splash of small waves was a peaceful sound, but then was drowned out by the motor roaring into life. The smell of gas and oil stung Tom's nose.

"Throw off the line," B.X. yelled over his shoulder.

The propeller bit in, bubbling the water. As they headed out under the stars, cold lake air swept over the boat. Tom shivered, thinking how upset his family must be. He was cold and tired and hungry, and a sense of terrible loneliness crept into his mind. What if they did kill him, what if he just disappeared like Dianne? The thought made tears come to his eyes.

9

"I say kill him."

Tom knelt under the open window of the cabin, listening to the argument between Red and B.X.

"And I say you're crazy," Red's voice answered. "You think I could put a bullet in that kid's head?"

"I'll do it."

Silence, then the smack of a fist hitting flesh and a crashing sound as someone fell to the floor.

"You aren't killing anyone, B.X.," Red said angrily.

Tom wanted to look through the window, but knew it would be suicide if he was seen. He was supposed to be at the far end of the island, fishing.

"I'm going to check the boat," Red said. "If anything happens to that kid, you're a dead man, B.X."

Tom ran to the woods that grew close to the cabin. Safe among the trees, he heard the cabin door slam, and saw Red walk down the path to the boathouse. Unlocking the door, he went inside.

Tom started toward the place where he had left Red's fishing rod; it was a very small island and he was there in a few minutes. He sat down on the big rock overlooking the deep water.

With a flick of the wrist, Tom cast the line. Sailing gracefully through the air, it fell into the water with a quiet plop. Tom let the line run deep, then reeled it in, watching for the beautiful sight of the spinner flashing up through the cold water.

Since arriving on the island, Tom had not seen a fish, but it was pleasant to sit in the sunshine and watch for signs of the police boat that he knew would be coming to his rescue. By now, the salesman would have told the police about Red, Tom, and the theft of his car, and before long they'd be searching the islands scattered across this huge lake.

When the spinner came dripping out of the water, Tom looked across the water. On the distant shore, a cabin cruiser moved past under the bright sun. Tom had seen many of the big boats go by, but they were always too far away for people to hear a shout for help.

*   *   *

The next afternoon Red returned to the island in the boat after being gone all day. He closed the boathouse door and locked it; the key was always on a thong around his neck. He carried two bags of food to the cabin, and the door slammed behind him.

Sneaking forward to an open window, Tom took out his notebook. Red and B.X. often quarrelled; Tom had picked up information, but nothing very useful. Dianne's location hadn't been mentioned.

Tom saw B.X. moodily carving a point on a wooden stick. Red was on the sofa, feet up. "I talked to our man in the ski mask," he said, "to be sure the Dorchester kid is getting fed okay. Then I met with O.L. He's going to send the Dorchester family a new ransom demand. If they don't cooperate this time, the girl will die."

Tom gasped in shock, then quickly scribbled the initials O.L. At last, some important information—another person was involved in the kidnapping!

"We reached an agreement," Red continued. "If any of us gets busted, we admit to nothing. Providing the cops don't arrest all of us, the ransom demands can continue. The money will be shared equally—including by anyone in prison."

B.X. stared at Red. "*Prison*?"

"Hey, relax. Nothing can go wrong."

Looking sulky, B.X. said no more. His moods could last for hours, so Tom closed the notebook and crept away. Somehow he must escape!

Following a trail through the trees he soon reached a rocky bluff overlooking the lake. In the distance was an island with a large house; he'd seen lights there at night, but how to alert the people?

There must be some way. Tom walked back and forth on the rocky beach, concentrating on the problem.

He felt like Robinson Crusoe, trapped forever on a desert island. He should put a note in a bottle advertising for a Man Friday. No—they might send Dietmar Oban by mistake.

Wait a minute. Wait a minute!

Tom grinned, pleased he'd thought of a way to escape at last. He hurried along the trail to the cabin. The sound of hammering came from the boathouse, where Red was trying to repair the leaky roof.

Creeping to the back of the cabin, Tom lifted the lid of the garbage can. He rooted around until he found the wine bottle that the two men had emptied during dinner last night, then pushed aside tin cans and sticky coffee grounds to find the cork.

Tom rushed back through the woods to the beach, where he got out the pen he had used to play battleships with Red, and then searched in his pockets for paper. Nothing. So who needs paper?

Pulling out his shirt tail, he ripped off a piece of cloth and stretched it over a flat rock.

Carefully, Tom printed: I AM PRISONER ON THE SMALL ISLAND WITH CABIN AND BOATHOUSE —TOM AUSTEN. He stuffed the cloth down the neck of the wine bottle and jammed the cork in place.

Tom lifted the bottle and threw it with all his might. It twisted in the air and splashed down, disappearing under the surface. His anxious eyes saw it reappear, bobbing like a cheerful little boat among the waves.

Which way would it go? The bottle seemed to hesitate, then got mixed up with some small waves and disappeared south. Tom crossed all his fingers and wished it luck before walking back to the cabin. He felt good.

Hammering still echoed in the clearing. Not wanting to share the cabin with B.X., Tom went into the boathouse. "Hi," he said to Red, who was standing at the top of a stepladder repairing a support beam.

"Hiya, kiddo," Red said, smiling. "How's the fishing?"

"I caught six pike, but I threw them back. Too small for me."

Red laughed. "That makes 54 imaginary pike you've caught this week. Beats my record for sure."

Sitting on the edge of the wooden planking, Tom dangled his feet above the water. "I'm bored," he said.

Red finished hammering a nail. "What did you say?"

"I'm bored."

"Want a game of checkers? I'm finished work now."

"No, thanks. You always win."

Climbing down the stepladder, Red sat beside Tom. "I get bored too, kiddo, but that's the way it goes."

Tom looked up at the man. "How come you're a criminal?"

Red shrugged. "I don't know."

"But there must be some reason," Tom insisted.

"Yeah, well, I guess it's for the excitement. Like on the train when you appeared and messed up all the plans. It was exciting to get away without being caught."

"But what if something had gone wrong? What if the conductor had started a fight, and you'd had to shoot him?"

Red was silent, looking down into the water that murmured around the boathouse supports.

"Have you ever killed anyone?"

Red smiled. "Sure have, kiddo."

Tom stared at the man, not sure if he was telling the truth. "I don't believe it," he said finally.

"There's a place in Saskatchewan called Moose Jaw," Red replied in a calm voice. "Three years ago, I held up the bank in Moose Jaw. As I came out the door, a police car stopped and a Mountie got out with a gun in her hand. I shot her right between the eyes."

Tom felt sick. He tried to look away from Red's face, but he couldn't.

"You see, kiddo, it's like a game. You kids play cops and robbers, right? Some of us just keep playing the game when we grow up. Your father decided to be a cop, and I decided to be a robber. It's still fun, just like being a kid."

"But we don't kill each other."

Red shrugged. "That's the way it goes. The Mountie was going to shoot me, so I plugged her first."

"But maybe she had kids!"

"So what? Nobody asked her to be a cop. Getting shot is part of the game."

Tom was silent. Now he realized what lay behind Red's easy smile.

He winked at Tom. "How about some checkers? I'll give you a two-man advantage."

"No, thanks," Tom muttered, looking down at the water.

"Don't be upset, kiddo. Life is tough. Now, come on, let's play some checkers."

"No," Tom said. "I don't like you anymore."

Red stared at him. Slowly, his face turned crimson. "Why? I like you, you're a nice kid. We've played checkers, and everything. I taught you to fish—it's not my fault you didn't catch anything. Why don't you like me?"

Tears rose in Tom's eyes. "You kill people! That's the most horrible thing I can imagine."

"Oh, so that's it." For a moment Red was silent. Then he shook his head, eyes sad. "You're lucky to be 11 years old. You wanna know why? Because you've still got a clean future ahead of you, anything's possible, you haven't made any major mistakes. If I could be young again, I'd do it differently." He waved toward the door. "Go on, beat it. I'm feeling tired."

The bright sunshine outside stung Tom's eyes, making tears run down his cheeks. He ran to the trail and followed it to the big rock, wishing he had never asked Red about being a criminal. Climbing up on the rock, Tom looked at Red's fishing rod lying in the sunshine. Impulsively, he picked it up and threw it into the lake, watching as the rod bubbled down through the water and disappeared.

He sat on the rock until night, going over and over the conversation in the boathouse. He listened for the sound of feet in the woods, hoping that Red would come and say that he was joking, but he had seen the man's eyes when he told Tom about killing the Mountie, and Tom knew the story was true.

At last, feeling tired and hungry, Tom went back to the cabin. The kerosene lamp was burning, throwing warm yellow light on the wooden walls and making the cabin feel comfortable.

B.X., as usual, was carving old sticks with his hunting knife. "Look who it is," he said, his voice sour.

"Hiya, kiddo." Red got up from his chair and went over to the wood stove. "Feel like some grub?"

Tom looked at the man's smiling face. How could he be so cheerful when he was a murderer?

"Ham and eggs and fried potatoes," Red said, "followed by coffee and doughnuts. What do you say, kiddo?"

"Okay, I guess," Tom said quietly. He went to the table and sat down. Butter sizzled in the frying pan, and the door of the stove banged as Red opened it to throw in more wood. Lowering his eyes, Tom slowly ran a finger back and forth on the table. He didn't want to eat but, when Red brought the food, he forced himself to have it all. He wasn't about to anger a killer.

* * *

The next morning, Tom woke up early. He lay in his sleeping bag, feeling sad, then put on his clothes and went outside.

The smell of the early morning air cheered him. Crossing the clearing, he started along the trail, thinking he might get lucky today and catch a pike. When he remembered the fishing rod was at the bottom of the lake, he stopped walking. His unhappiness felt like a lump of rock in his stomach.

He had to get off the island! What about the bottle? Tom started toward the south end of the island, hoping for some sign that help was on its way.

He came out of the woods and stopped. The lake was magnificent, with a soft white mist floating above its surface. The sun was low in the sky, burning huge and red behind the mist, while somewhere in the distance a bird was calling. Tom walked down to the shore. As he stood on the rocky beach, he saw a bottle rolling gently back and forth between tiny waves at the edge of the water.

The cork came loose with a *pfffft*, revealing a piece of cloth inside. It was damp, and the ink had smudged, but he was able to read that Tom Austen was a prisoner on the small island with cabin and boathouse.

In sudden anger, Tom flung the bottle out over the lake. It smacked into the water, ruining the calm of the morning. Now Tom knew he was really trapped, alone on the island with two men, one of them a killer and the other probably worse. He decided to swim for it, then realized that was crazy. The lake was too wide, the water colder than cold.

What, then?

There was one possibility. Earlier, it had seemed a dirty trick to play on Red, but now Tom didn't care. He walked back and forth on the beach, thinking about the plan. It was taking a chance, but he had to get off the island.

Tom returned to the cabin. He opened the door cautiously, hoping the two men were still asleep in their bunk beds. He listened for their deep breathing, then tiptoed around collecting the kerosene lamp, matches, and a can with extra kerosene.

Tom followed the trail to the big rock, where the

island was narrowest. Pouring some kerosene on the underbrush, he began to make a trail of fuel. Soon the island was cut in half by the smelly kerosene.

Tom looked toward the distant shore, where a big cabin cruiser lay at anchor. There was no sign that anyone was awake on the boat, but Tom couldn't wait. Lighting a match, he tossed it into the kerosene. There was a *poof!* and the flames shot across the fuel, eating into the dead wood of the underbrush.

Tom jumped back, startled by the fury he had released. The fire was everywhere at once, burning the kerosene by the big rock and rushing along the line of fuel that divided the island. The burning wood crackled, and hot flames jumped from branch to branch among the low bushes, reaching up to the bark on the big trees.

The heat made Tom sweat. He wished he could put the fire back inside the match. Climbing quickly onto the big rock, he looked at the white and black smoke twisting thickly into the air.

Nobody had appeared on the cabin cruiser. Idiots! The fire was roaring among the high branches of the trees. How could anything spread so quickly? The island was already cut in half and now the flames were eating in two directions, toward the south, and toward the north, where the cabin waited.

"Red," Tom shouted. "Red and B.X., watch out!"

But his words were carried away among the clouds of smoke. Tom tried again, screaming his warning, but he knew it was hopeless. The heat was unbearable—he jumped from the rock and staggered onto the rocky beach with sweat dripping from his face.

Across the lake, a speedboat was rushing toward him.

Tom wiped the sweat out of his eyes and looked again, sure he had made a mistake. But the boat was still coming fast. Waving his arms, he waded into the lake until it was up to his waist. He looked at the fire crackling through the trees, then turned to wave again. A man in the boat waved back, as the engine noise grew above the roaring of the flames.

"Help," Tom shouted, wading deeper. The waves glowed orange, reflecting the inferno above. The boat slowed as it approached. Two men were inside, one still wearing his pyjamas. As he helped Tom into the speedboat, it veered sharply away from the fire.

"Two men are on the island," Tom cried. "Around the other side, at the cabin. Hurry!"

The man at the wheel opened up the power. He glanced back at Tom. "What happened? What caused the fire?"

"I did," Tom said. "Those guys are criminals—they kidnapped me and Dianne Dorchester."

The man looked amazed. "You're one of the kidnapped kids? You mean, we're going to be heroes?"

"Sure," Tom replied, "but first you've got to capture Red and B.X. They've got a gun."

The men looked at each other.

"It's true," Tom exclaimed. "They've kept me prisoner on that island."

The man in the pyjamas looked at Tom. "You sure about that gun?"

"Yes."

"Okay."

He moved to the bow. Tom felt the wind on his face as the boat skimmed forward across the water; he looked at the terrible fire he had caused, then put his head down. At least he was safe.

"Are those the guys, sonny?"

Red and B.X. were on the tiny pier in front of the cabin, waving their arms and shouting. Tom wondered why they hadn't escaped, then saw the smoking ruins of the boathouse.

When they were close enough to see the fear on the faces of Red and B.X., the man slowed the boat.

"Help," Red yelled. "Come on, help us!"

"Yeah, help," B.X. called, staring fearfully at the flames that jumped toward the pier where he stood with Red.

The man at the steering wheel cupped his hands around his mouth. "Throw us your gun!"

"What gun?" Red held up his empty hands. "Come on, save us!"

"Throw your gun to us," the man repeated.

Flames shone on B.X.'s sweaty face as he said something to Red and pointed at the fire. Red shook his head.

"All right, boys," the man at the wheel shouted, revving the engine. "You can stay and fry!"

"Stop!" B.X. grabbed Red's shirt with both hands. For a second, it looked as if he was going to throw the bigger man into the lake, but then Red knocked B.X.'s hands away and turned toward the speedboat.

"Okay," he shouted, "you win."

There was a pause in which Red stared at Tom, and then he reached inside his shirt to the shoulder holster. The black revolver appeared in his hand and sailed through the air, dropping with a clunk into the bottom of the boat. The man in pyjamas picked it up.

The boat moved in quickly to get Red and B.X. "No tricks now," the man warned, covering Red and B.X. with the gun as they climbed into the boat, "or we'll throw you both overboard."

Red laughed. "Sure thing, Mr. Pyjamas." Turning, he winked at Tom. "Well, kiddo, I take off my hat to you. When it comes to cops and robbers, you're a better player than me."

Tom looked up at the man's blue eyes, but he couldn't smile.

10

Although Red and B.X. were soon under arrest, the case was not closed. The man in the ski mask remained at large, Dianne was still missing, and the police had been unable to locate the mysterious kidnapper known only as O.L.

The city's two rivers had risen higher and higher, swollen by heavy rains and runoff water from winter snows. Now they were close to flooding, despite the hundreds of sandbags that had been piled on top of the dikes along the riverbanks. Those areas of Winnipeg threatened with flooding had been evacuated. No one was supposed to be there, but Tom had decided he couldn't miss the excitement.

Heavy rain soaked him as he walked along a street of

deserted houses before turning onto a main road that ran straight to the Assiniboine. At the end of the street was the strange and thrilling sight of a bridge almost covered by the raging waters of the river; sandbags had been heaped across the road, cutting off the flooded bridge.

A terrible grinding sound filled the air. The metal girders of the bridge were heaving under the pressure of the water. If the bridge collapsed it might tear a hole in the dike, flooding everything.

The evacuated neighborhood was an eerie sight. Rain-soaked plywood covered the windows of stores; houses and apartment buildings were entirely dark. The streets were empty of cars, empty of people.

Headlights shone in the distance. Tom crouched behind a garbage can, watching a car approach through the pounding rain. It stopped in front of an old apartment building, and Mr. Stones stepped out.

The teacher walked quickly to the building, carrying a pizza container. Going inside, he was swallowed by the gloom.

More headlights shone in the distance: a police car, moving fast. It swerved to a stop by the curb, then Officer Larson leapt out and ran swiftly inside.

What was going on?

Tom hurried through the cold rain to the building. The door was unlocked; he stepped into a lobby containing some old furniture and a row of mailboxes on the wall. There was one elevator, but it failed to respond when Tom pressed the button. Pushing open a door, he stepped cautiously into a narrow hallway. Stairs led up.

Tom climbed slowly, his hand on a cold railing. He heard nothing except the beating of rain against the building and the distant grinding of the bridge under the river's pressure.

Then, he heard voices.

Creeping higher, Tom cautiously stepped into a dark hallway. Faint light showed under the door of an apartment. He moved closer, hardly daring to breathe. Now he clearly heard the voices of Officer Larson and Mr. Stones.

"Where *is* he?" Mr. Stones said. His voice was ragged, hoarse, horrible. "He's late!"

"Calm down," Officer Larson replied. He sounded grumpier than usual. "In a few more minutes we'll be rich. But don't forget, there's an equal share for Red and B.X."

"I don't want your money," Mr. Stones cried. "I want my sanity! I want to be free of your terrible threats to my family. I want Dianne to go home again. I want my life to be back to normal!"

"That will never happen," said Officer Larson. "You'd better escape into hiding, then change your identity. That's what I plan to do."

"I was blackmailed into helping your scheme! My family was threatened."

"Quit bleating. I've heard it all before."

"Why have you done this? *Why*?"

"For money, what else? I don't make enough as a cop."

"Rubbish!"

"It was a lucky break when my investigation of the kidnapping led me to Red. I demanded to be included in his conspiracy, or I'd bust him. This will make me rich forever."

Tom was desperately scribbling in his notebook. Somehow he must get help, fast. He began moving away from the door, and then suddenly stopped.

Someone was climbing the staircase.

*   *   *

Tom's eyes darted back and forth in search of hiding. Nothing. He crouched against the wall, listening fearfully to the footsteps on the creaking stairs. A man appeared, wearing an expensive hat and overcoat.

Mr. Dorchester.

Tom was so thrilled to see Dianne's father that he jumped up from hiding, a big smile on his face. But this startled Mr. Dorchester, who yelled in shock.

Immediately the apartment door swung open, revealing the orange glow of candlelight. Officer Larson stood in the doorway, gun in hand.

"Tom Austen—I might have known. Get in here, you little meddler. Dorchester, bring that ransom into the apartment. Move it!"

With a heavy heart, Tom stepped into the apartment. The bridge outside swayed back and forth, gripped by the powerful water surging past. Mr. Stones sat on a frayed sofa, tears streaming down his face. Yellow candlelight shone on Dianne, who stood at the kitchen counter with pizza in her hand and a look of utter astonishment on her face.

"Tom," she cried, running to him with open arms.

As they hugged she saw her father, and rushed to hold him. Her skin was pale and there were dark smudges under her eyes.

Tom looked at his teacher. "Why'd you do it, sir?"

"They threatened to hurt my family, Tom. Someone Dianne trusted was needed to drive the kidnap van. Red and B.X. were hiding in the back. They put Dianne out with a needle while I drove to this apartment they'd rented."

"Didn't anyone see her being brought in?"

"She was in a wheelchair, wearing a grey wig and a shawl. She looked like someone's grandmother, sound asleep in her chair." He turned to Dianne. "Please forgive me."

She hugged him. "You had no choice, Mr. Stones. Thanks for bringing me pizza."

Mr. Dorchester handed an attache case to Officer Larson. "Here's your money. It's all there, in cash. Count it if you must, but I'm a man of my word."

Tom walked into the kitchen. "Okay to have some pizza?" he asked Officer Larson.

"I guess so." He checked the contents of the attache case, then closed it. "Tomorrow I'll be on a tropical beach, enjoying my sudden retirement from the police force. I hated saluting officers like Tom's conceited father."

Tom came out of the kitchen, eating a slab of pizza. In his hand was a candle. Walking toward Officer Larson, he said, "Want a bite? This tastes great!"

Officer Larson pointed his revolver at Tom. "Don't try anything."

Tom thrust the pizza at Officer Larson. As the man

tried to push it away, Tom tilted the candle. Hot wax fell on Officer Larson's hand. Shouting in pain, he dropped the gun.

"Get it, sir," Tom cried, kicking the revolver toward Mr. Stones.

Officer Larson grabbed the attache case, broke for the door and disappeared down the stairs. "So long, suckers," he yelled. At the same moment, the building shook as the bridge outside collapsed. Ugly brown water surged through a hole in the dike and rolled down the street toward them.

"Bring the gun," Tom shouted to Mr. Stones.

The wood of the old building groaned as it was struck by the river. Reaching the stairs, Tom saw water gushing and roaring below. Officer Larson, clutching the attache case, stood watching the flood that blocked his escape.

With Mr. Stones pointing Officer Larson's own revolver at him, the disgraced policeman slowly climbed the stairs and handed the attache case to Dianne's father.

"I surrender," Officer Larson said bleakly. "I was a fool."

Tom looked out the window. "The flood's covered your cars! But I see police out in boats—let's signal for help."

Mr. Dorchester hugged Dianne again. "I'm so glad you're safe, sweetheart. Your mother will be thrilled. We've missed you so much."

"Wasn't Tom splendid, saving us all from being shot?" Dianne smiled at him. "Thank you," she said quietly. "You were wonderful."

11

As the flood waters receded, the safe return of Dianne Dorchester provided citizens with welcome news. The front page of the newspaper featured a huge picture of Tom, grinning under a headline that said: HERO OF THE YEAR!

Dianne was recovering in hospital from her ordeal. When Tom arrived for his first visit with her, the room was jammed with people. Reporters from the media were there, along with doctors and nurses, Dianne's parents, even patients from other wards of the hospital. As Tom entered the room, he felt all their eyes staring, waiting to hear what he and Dianne would say. So they said nothing and just smiled at each other, knowing they could talk when the world had gone away.

The newspaper photographer asked Tom to put his arm around Dianne and give her a smile. The next day, the picture was on the front page of the newspaper with a story saying that Dianne would soon be out of hospital. A few days later, Tom was surprised to receive in the mail an envelope marked "Tom Austen, c/o City Police, Winnipeg, Manitoba". A Montreal woman enclosed a picture of Tom and Dianne clipped from *Le Devoir* newspaper, and a letter saying what a wonderful boy Tom must be. A girl wrote from New Orleans to say she wanted to marry Tom as soon as possible.

Each night after dinner, the family filled their scrapbook with newspaper clippings and Tom's fan mail. "This is getting ridiculous," Liz grumbled as she labored over a huge newspaper headline from Scotland. "My brother's not *this* big a hero." She looked at him. "I could do detective work. I bet it's easy."

Tom laughed. "It requires a redhead's superior brainpower."

Liz's dark eyes studied him. "Those are challenging words, dear brother. I think I'll start looking for clients."

*   *   *

Before life returned to normal at Queenston School, there was a special event. Late in May, Tom and the others decorated their classroom with banners reading *Welcome to Kids Day, Part Two!!* and *Welcome Back, Dianne*.

It was great to see Dianne back in the classroom, talking happily to Mr. Stones. The teacher had not been charged with kidnapping because of Red's threats against his family. The Dorchester family had urged the authorities to let Mr. Stones continue his work at Queenston School, and the teacher had returned to his classroom.

The second celebration of Kids Day went well, with large quantities of ice cream and lemonade quickly evaporating. Pete Tyler was there and spent some time talking to Tom. "I've never liked having my picture taken," he explained, "because of my criminal past. Cameras have depressed me ever since I had mug shots taken at the police station when I was arrested."

"Were you ever a kidnapper?" Tom asked. "I thought maybe you were the man in the ski mask."

Pete shook his head. "When I was young, I stole cars for cheap thrills. Then I ended up behind bars. A criminal record makes things tough—I'm lucky to have this job. Mr. Dorchester turned me down for work at his estate, which really upset me, but that's life, I guess."

After talking to everyone else, Tom got a chance to speak to Mr. Stones.

"I should have figured out you were feeding Dianne, sir. In class you had receipts from *Pizza Perfect* but pizza gives you heartburn. The food must have been for someone else, and we all know Dianne loves pizza." Tom smiled. "You made another mistake, sir. Remember in the principal's office, when I first described Dianne being kidnapped? I didn't say the van was brown, but afterwards in the classroom you mentioned its color. As Red would say, you're not very good at the game of cops and robbers."

"It's not a game, Tom, I've learned that. I'm just glad everyone's safe."

Next, Tom talked to Dietmar Oban. "I've got the poems I promised you. They're excellent, real heartbreakers. I should charge you money."

"Forget it, Austen." Dietmar snatched the poems from his hand. "Jumping from the catwalk at that warehouse was the worst experience of my life. I deserve these poems."

Dietmar crossed the room to Elizabeth Whitman, who stood by herself near the windows, sipping lemonade. Sunlight glowed in her dark hair as she read the poems. Now Tom wished he'd given Elizabeth the poems himself, but it was too late for that.

Mr. Nicholson came into the classroom and called Tom forward. "I'm pleased to announce you're the new captain of the school patrol." As everyone applauded, he presented Tom with a patrol belt. "I predict a brilliant future for you as a detective. Perhaps one day you'll write about your adventures."

"If I do," Tom grinned, "I'll call this one the Case of the Golden Boy."

When the principal was gone, Dianne came over to Tom. Up close, her eyes were very blue. "Congratulations, Tom. I never told you before, but you look handsome in your patrol belt."

He blushed. "Really?"

"Yes." Dianne smiled. "I'm looking forward to passing your corner after school today. Maybe you could read me one of your poems."

She brushed his cheek with a kiss. "You're my hero, Tom."

It was the best moment of his life—so far.

**Eric Wilson
at Ilihakvik School, Cambridge Bay**

Eric Wilson's main advice to young writers is, "Use what you know," so it's no surprise that Tom Austen has a huge enthusiasm for the Hardy Boys and a taste for adventure. That's because he's modeled on Eric, whose childhood memories of a major Winnipeg flood inspired some ideas for this first Tom Austen mystery.

DISNEYLAND HOSTAGE
A Liz Austen Mystery

Eric Wilson

Renfield held a wriggling, hairy tarantula in his hand. Suddenly the maniac cackled, and ran straight at me with the giant spider!

Facing a tarantula is just one of the exciting, suspenseful moments that Liz Austen experiences in DISNEYLAND HOSTAGE. On her own during a California holiday, unable to seek the help of her brother Tom, she is plunged into the middle of an international plot when a boy named Ramón disappears from his room at the Disneyland Hotel. Has Ramón been taken hostage? Before Liz can answer that question, her own safety is threatened when terrorists strike at the most unlikely possible target: Disneyland itself.

THE ICE DIAMOND QUEST

A Tom and Liz Austen Mystery

Eric Wilson

As a flare lit the night, the sea turned crimson. In the bright light, they saw a powerful yacht. On its bridge, a signal light began to flash.

Why is this mysterious yacht flashing a signal off the coast of Newfoundland on a cold November evening? Tom and Liz Austen, with their cousins Sarah and Duncan Joy, follow a difficult trail toward the truth. As they search, people known as the Hawk and the Renegades cause major problems, but the cousins press on. Then, in the darkness of an abandoned mine and later on stormy seas, they face together the greatest dangers ever.

COLD MIDNIGHT IN VIEUX QUÉBEC

A Tom Austen Mystery

Eric Wilson

Fireworks exploded into the sky above the Ice Palace as Tom struggled forward through the throngs of people, then was suddenly grabbed by a big police officer.

"Tu ne peux pas aller là-bas. That is a security zone."

"You've got to let me get past," Tom shouted.

The leaders of the world's superpowers have agreed to meet in Québec City to put an end to chemical weapons — but powerful forces will stop at nothing to prevent the agreement from being signed. From the first chilling page, you will be gripped by suspense as you follow Tom Austen and Dietmar Oban through the ancient, mysterious streets of Vieux Québec in quest of world peace.

CODE RED AT THE SUPERMALL

A Tom and Liz Austen Mystery

Eric Wilson

They swam past gently moving strands of sea-weed and pieces of jagged coral, then Tom almost choked in horror. A shark was coming straight at him, ready to strike.

Have you ever visited a shopping mall that has sharks and piranhas, a triple-loop rollercoaster, 22 waterslides, an Ice Palace, submarines, 828 stores, and a major mystery to solve? Soon after Tom and Liz Austen arrive at the West Edmonton Mall, a bomber strikes and they must follow a trail that leads through the fabled splendors of the supermall to hidden danger.

THE GREEN GABLES DETECTIVES

A Liz Austen Mystery

Eric Wilson

I almost expected to see Anne signalling to Diana from her bedroom window as we climbed the slope towards Green Gables, then Makiko grabbed my arm. "Danger!"

Staring at the house, I saw a dim shape slip around a corner into hiding. "Who's there?" I called. "We see you!"

While visiting the famous farmhouse known as Green Gables, Liz Austen and her friends are swept up in baffling events that lead from an ancient cemetery to a haunted church, and then a heart-stopping showdown in a deserted lighthouse as fog swirls across Prince Edward Island. Be prepared for eerie events and unbearable suspense as you join the Green Gables detectives for a thrilling adventure.

SPIRIT IN THE RAINFOREST
A Tom and Liz Austen Mystery

Eric Wilson

The branches trembled, then something slipped away into the darkness of the forest. "That was Mosquito Joe!" Tom exclaimed.

"Or his spirit," Liz said. "Let's get out of here."

The rainforest of British Columbia holds many secrets, but none stranger than those of Nearby Island. After hair-raising events during a Pacific storm, Tom and Liz Austen seek answers among the island's looming trees. Alarmed by the ghostly shape of the hermit Mosquito Joe, they look for shelter in a deserted school in the rainforest. Then, in the night, Tom and Liz hear a girl's voice crying *Beware! Beware!*

VAMPIRES OF OTTAWA
A Liz Austen Mystery

Eric Wilson

Suddenly the vampire rose up from behind a tombstone and fled, looking like an enormous bat with his black cape streaming behind in the moonlight.

Within the walls of a gloomy estate known as Blackwater, Liz Austen discovers the strange world of Baron Nicolai Zaba, a man who lives in constant fear. What is the secret of the ancient chapel's underground vault? Why are the words *In Evil Memory* scrawled on a wall? Who secretly threatens the Baron? All the answers lie within these pages but be warned: *reading this book will make your blood run cold.*

THE KOOTENAY KIDNAPPER

A Tom Austen Mystery

Eric Wilson

Only groans and creaks sounded from the old building as it waited for Tom to discover its secret. With a rapidly-beating heart, he approached the staircase...

What is the secret lurking in the ruins of the lonely ghost town in the mountains of British Columbia? Solving this mystery is only one of the challenges facing Tom Austen after he arrives in B.C. with his sidekick, Dietmar Oban, and learns that a young girl has disappeared without a trace. Then a boy is kidnapped, and electrifying events quickly carry Tom to a breathtaking climax deep underground in Cody Caves, where it is forever night...